WHIMS
OF THE
WICKED

REBECCA GREY

Potential Triggers

Please read responsibly. While Whims of the Wicked has intentionally been written as a fun and (mostly) sweet holiday read there are mentions of:

Loss of a parent (mother)

Sexual harassment

Attempted *and* successful robbery (without weapons)

Self deprecating internal dialogue

Mild physical violence (ex: bar fight)

Please be mindful while reading.

To my Hallmark movie loving 'spiritual' mother, Laquita. I wish I could send you a copy in heaven.

Contents

SONNET

One might think that because we are lesser fairies, our courts would not be as vicious as the High Fae, but they'd be wrong. Very wrong. Especially for any fairy like me; born with the pointed ears of the Fae with the same long lanky body but significantly less magic. Without any magic, actually.

Thinking of my impending return to society, sweat coats my palms and then almost immediately turns to ice as a winter wind shoots down the dirt path and rustles my cloak. Thick parchment crinkles in my hand as I fist my fingers around it. The first snow of winter drifts down from the fluffy gray clouds that loom over Bitten Woods. Between the rustle of bare branches, a clacking noise begins to rise. Large beastly flowers snap their toothy mouths toward the movement of the flakes lazily falling toward them. The woods are full of danger, but never as badly as at night when the flowers and trees show their fangs.

Carefully, I open the folded bit of paper to glance down at my list and angle myself away from the edges of the path. This portion of trees hasn't gotten its name because the plants are particularly kind. Flowers bloom all year round in our little town of Daydale, but the most beautiful plants here are cruel if one gets too close. Ignoring the flurry of movement on either side of me as a large hydrangea straightens to catch snow with a snap of its jaw, I mentally tick through my plan to save Yule from being an utter disaster. This will be the first Yule without Mother and after everything my family has gone through, we deserve the best holiday imaginable.

Thus, my plan was hatched. First, I will be attending the Hollis' ball, the start of the many events that countdown to Yule. An invite, one of the few simple tasks on my list, is almost guaranteed since Trudy is a long-time friend. This party will be my opportunity to show everyone in the Court of Frost that I'm not some magicless broken thing to be pitied and avoided. Because that's what people have done since we lost mother. Avoided us. Without her, we fell from our standing and lost whatever support we might have been given. Obviously, I'm not bitter about it or anything. That is how court works after all. Okay, maybe I'm a tad bitter. Because, how dare they kick us when we were already down? Father and Merry—my little sister—did not deserve to be treated like that while we were mourning. And neither did I.

Anyway—I'm getting off track here—I'll attend the Harlows' ball where I plan to be so absolutely charming and not-at-all-broken that I catch the attention of Cassius Calloway. The quintessential golden boy. The most eligible bachelor in Daydale. The heir of the hottest and most powerful family in our lesser court. The Calloways always host the largest, most exclusive party of the year, the Yuletide Ball. I've never been invited before, but I've only been old enough to attend such events for a year, and six months of that have been spent garbed in black dresses and closed up in the tiny shack we call a home.

Achieving an invitation to such a party makes the rest of my list seem almost easy. Sure, I'd need a date to the Yuletide Ball, but once I got my hands on an invitation, men would line up to take me. That is if Cassius himself hasn't already fallen head over heels for me. And why wouldn't he? I'm great. Then all I need to make this the perfect Yule would be to get a kiss under the mistletoe and take whatever savings I have managed to gather since starting my work with Dr. Lowen to buy my sister and father a gift.

This is a doable list. Right? Yes. I *can* do this. I will do this.

For Merry. For Father. For Mother, may her soul forever rest in peace. For me.

While Mother passed down her stick-straight black hair, blue eyes, and button nose, she didn't pass down so much as a lick of her power. Which is really such a shame when magic is what grants standing in court. Now, six months since her passing, I'm expected to shed my mourning clothes and return to high society. The place where gossip could ruin you and parties brimming with power-hungry mothers and their practically vampiric daughters looking to find husbands loom around every corner. *Scary.* Not only should I return, but I am also supposed to be one of them. Or should attempt to be at the very least. Though I doubt very much I'll find a husband. With no magic, no fangs, and no conniving mother at my side, I might very well be eaten alive. My father is nothing more than an out-of-work blacksmith with a bad back. My sister...well, as wonderful as Merry is, she's shown no signs of having our mother's gifts.

I let out a long sigh, my breath clouding in front of my face, as I fold the parchment. I can do this, I remind myself. I can wow them all. And society be damned, I can do it all without any magic.

At my left, a large blue tulip arches toward me, smiling to reveal its pointed teeth before attempting to take a bite out of my skirt. I bat the plant away. At the age of twenty, I've walked through these woods with only the light of the moon to guide my steps home more and more frequently. The flowers aren't so bad as long as you stay out of their reach.

Clutching my bag in one hand and my list in the other, I trudge through the snow that's begun to gather in a thin layer over the dirt. White clusters of flakes cling to my curling fringe and the length of my hair piled on top of my head. I try to shake the snow off only for it to double its vigor as the clouds open up. Pebbles crunch under my boots. I squint to try and see where the path curves ahead and find a lump stretched out across my path, only yards away.

What is *that*?

My eyes narrow as if that might enhance my eyesight. It does nothing of the like and the lump remains only a lump. I stop. How peculiar. Maybe someone lost something from their carriage or wagon as they drove through? Could it be an animal? Or—

A groan of pain comes from the shape that is now very decidedly a man.

Great. Perfect. Just what I want when I'm already exhausted and my fingers feel like ice.

Still, my pulse ticks faster. My heart threatens to leap up into my throat. Someone is hurt, possibly left for dead where so few traverse. Honestly, they are lucky that I even stumbled upon them at all.

Hurrying forward toward the man, I ignore the blisters on the back of my feet that feel as though they'll rub open. Excess fabric from my skirt sways and flicks until I hiss and clutch the material as I run.

"Sir? Are you injured?" Cold seeps through my many layers as I drop down onto my knees at his side. I'm far from trained, but I can hold a bandage to a bleeding wound and act as a crutch until I get him where he needs to be. Dr. Lowen's office is only a ten-minute walk back in the other direction.

The man lies on his side, curled tightly into himself, his large muscular body nearly double the size of mine. I blink down at his all-black attire, spotted with white snow that melts almost as soon as it lands. Reaching, I grunt as I roll his body toward me. Even his hair is black—no, not hair. A hat?

My brows pinch. He turns. A black mask is

pulled over his head, only revealing golden brown eyes. In the next breath, his hand curls around my throat, not enough pressure to cut off my airflow, but enough to hold me still. Goosebumps form along my flesh. Can he feel my increasing pulse underneath his thumb that strokes along my skin? Not a single callous mars his fingers, his skin somehow still so soft against mine.

"Give me all the coin you've got in that bag of yours and you'll be free to go." Low and rough, his voice sends a shiver down my spine.

Am I being robbed right now? Of course I am. Just the cherry on top of an already terrible six months.

Narrowing my gaze on his, I stiffen. There are coins in my bag. A week's pay for my work, but I need that money to buy my family Yule gifts and help supplement Father's income. I'll be damned if he thinks I'm going to hand that over. Who is this terror that thought to rob a woman blind on her way home? What an absolute asshole. Like a storybook villain, this one.

So I do the only thing I can think to do. I grip the straps of my bag, thankfully heavy with my latest read, and swing it with every ounce of strength right into his head. The hit lands with a satisfying slap.

His hand releases me. Success! Sucking in a

steadying breath, I harness the rush of anger at the stranger for trying to fool me and swing again. And again. And again. Then again for good measure. I beat him as though he is little more than a rug needing the dust knocked out of it. Truly, I should consider doing some sort of sport because I've got an impressive swing.

"How dare you!" I seethe, standing for better leverage. "Trying to rob a woman on her way home. You're nothing more than..." I truly can't find an insult fitting enough and settle on, "than a rat!"

He grunts at a particularly well-aimed shot to his gut. Go me! His arms windmill wildly to take hold of my bag. The hit I managed to take at his head has spun his black mask enough that his eyes are now covered. If I wasn't so furious I might laugh. Next, I'll aim for his groin. That will show him.

"Stop! Stop, woman, stop!" he growls, finally snatching up one of my wrists.

But if I am to be attacked and robbed, I deserve to see the face of the offender. With my one free hand, I stretch to grab the material atop his head, far finer than I expected it to be, and pull it away. Tufts of hair as white as the snow stick out at all angles around his pointed ears. Full lips spread into a sneer somehow accentuating his high cheekbones and youthful face. He's beautiful. And he's...familiar.

Oh no.

Gasping, I grip the mask. The thief who has come to rob me is none other than Malcom Black. I've never gotten close to the man, but I know him from a distance. His family is one of the three richest and most powerful in the Court of Frost. Right alongside the Calloways.

So why is he here trying to take my money?

"You're a feral little thing, aren't you?" He expels a long breath, eyes searching my face with no glint of recognition in them. He truly doesn't know who I am. And why would he? I'm basically a no one.

"You tried to rob me," I manage to answer after several heartbeats. My pulse has risen to the quickness of a hummingbird's wings. Malcom Black. Malcom Black. MALCOM-FUCKING-BLACK is here gripping my wrist and scowling at me.

"Well, now that you've seen my face, I doubt I'll be doing much of that." Those brown eyes dart to the mask still clutched in my hand, slide to my face, then down my body mostly hidden by the modest garb I wear for work, then to my wrist still circled within his grasp. One by one, he lifts his fingers from my skin as though he's disgusted to have ever touched me. "You've got an arm on you; I'll give you that. What, are you a female boxer?"

"A secretary, actually. I'm so sorry. If I'd known it was you..."

"You'd have given me all of your coin?" His large hands sweep down his well-fitted black shirt and trousers brushing away debris and melting snowflakes.

How did he manage to lie on the ground with no cloak or coat to keep him warm? How long did he wait for someone to amble down this path?

"No," I say, firmly, but maybe I wouldn't have hit him hard enough to turn the side of his perfectly handsome face that brilliant shade of red. My own cheeks must be flushed a similar color because heat rushes underneath my skin as embarrassment floods me. I crane my neck to look up at him fully. Goodness, he is tall. "Why, might I ask, are you trying to rob me?"

"Tried," he corrects. "Tried and failed." His shoulders drop and almost curl. "This was a terrible idea. I—" He pinches his nose rushing through his words. "I'm a fool who lost a great deal in gambling and am trying to make up that debt before my father notices and cuts me off."

Malcom Black, the second richest and most eligible bachelor in Daydale, has resorted to robbery to accommodate his debt. How much could he have possibly lost to gambling? Likely a far greater number than even I can imagine.

"So you've resorted to taking women's purses, Mr. Black?" I almost snort at the absurdity of this entire situation. "I should swing at you again for such a terrible idea. And then again because you were so terrifically bad at it. If you can't take a hit, then you shouldn't have tried at all." But I won't hit him again. Even if I want to. Because this is *Malcom Black* for crying out loud.

I lift my bag and he flinches, though I've only brought it closer to my chest to clutch tighter. Just in case he works up the courage to try again.

"And you could've done better?" he accuses, rubbing at his red cheek.

"Yes." I plant my hands on my hips. "In fact, I would have. You left yourself wide open for that hit. You should have come up from behind me to limit my range of motion instead of this foul act."

Wonderful. Now I'm giving him tips on how to steal.

Shut up, Sonnet. Just shut up.

"I'll keep that in mind for next time. What do you keep in that bag of yours anyway? It hurts like the dickens."

I give him my best sheepish grin before plucking out the thick hardbound book. "Poetry."

"Just my luck to run into a well-read woman. And your name?"

"I'm not in the habit of sharing my name with men who try to steal from me."

And maybe if he doesn't know my name, we can forget this entire thing ever happened.

"Well, my apology would not be good enough if I did not address it to you directly." He folds his arms over his wide chest, the pose showing off the powerful curve of his biceps. Damn, this man is beautiful. Terrible. Annoying. And absolutely handsome. If he'd wanted to hurt me he could have. It would have been nothing to him to manhandle the bag away from me. That has to count for something, doesn't it?

"Sonnet. Sonnet Weatherwood."

He nods and looks me up and down as if to see if that name fits me. Then he nods again. I shift my weight from foot to foot, uneasy at the heaviness of his judgment. Yet, I wasn't the one who had tried to commit a crime. Why should I care what he thinks of me? I straighten, holding my chin high. Yes, even though he is who he is, he should be ashamed of what has taken place here. No true gentleman would ever be caught participating in such a terrible thing.

Or maybe Malcom Black isn't a gentleman at all.

Malcom looks down at his feet and cocks his

head. I catch the familiar crinkle of parchment as he takes a step back and plucks none other than my list for Yule up off the ground. My cheeks go from warm to burning and the sensation dips down to my chest and rises all the way to my ears. In my haste for self-preservation, I'd managed to drop my list.

No. No...*No*. This cannot be happening to me.

"What is this?" he mumbles.

"I dropped that. I'll take it back now." I lunge for the list.

He lifts his arm out of my reach. "Interesting."

"Hardly. Now give it back." My voice betrays me in its strain. Because of course it does. Can't even trust my own body to have my back.

Malcom arches a brow and begins unfolding the parchment.

"*Interesting*," he repeats as a wolf-like smile spreads across his gorgeous face.

Malcom

Aren't women supposed to be quiet docile creatures? I've never known one to be quite as untamed as the one who now glares up at me with the ferocity of a wild cat. Or perhaps all women have such a creature below their skin and the niceties are a clever disguise.

Sonnet Weatherwood. The irony of her name being Sonnet and her cracking me across the jaw with a book of poetry is not lost on me. My little *Poesy*, here, is something to keep an eye on. Someone I find myself wanting to keep an eye on as I soak in the interest and beauty of her features. I want for very little and what I do want I tend to get.

Her weathered parchment crinkles even as it dampens when large flakes of snow fall upon it. I unfold it, managing to keep it out of her reach despite her efforts. Though it isn't hard. She is quite a short beastly thing. The scroll of fine feminine writing loops across the page. A list with dainty hearts and drawings of mistletoe decorates the edges. How...*adorable*. I scowl.

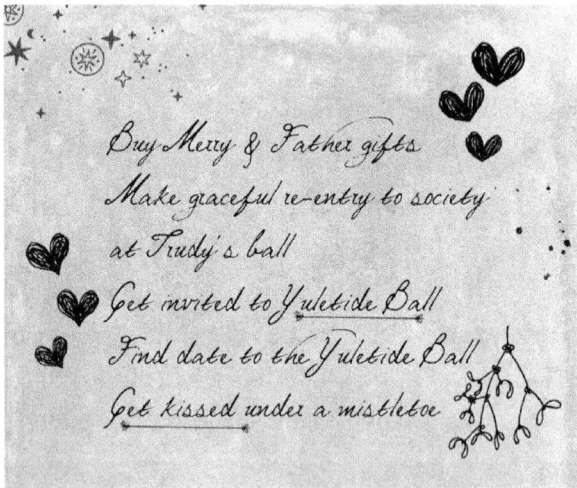

Buy Merry & Father gifts

Make graceful re-entry to society at Trudy's ball

Get invited to Yuletide Ball

Find date to the Yuletide Ball

Get kissed under a mistletoe

My eyes darted from the paper to her face. Strands of her dark hair have fallen around her features, framing startlingly blue eyes. Blue as bright as a cloudless sky on a sunny day. Blue as thunderous as the ocean as it beats against the shore. Blue so icy and filled with hate that I can't help but hold her gaze a second longer than necessary. All of this meets in the swirl of color within her irises. A blush across her cheeks makes her eyes that much more vibrant. She is a pretty girl, a bit plain in her dress, but even I can admit to finding everything else about her quite attractive. If one could be attracted to wild animals, that is.

For once in my life, everything may be aligning for me. This woman...this list... is exactly what I need. It's a steppingstone to fixing my problems; all I need to do is charm—manipulate—my way to an advantage. She even said herself she could rob someone better than me. So I should let her. And in exchange, I'll help her with this holiday list of hers.

Getting a date for her events shouldn't be too hard, but an invite to the Yuletide Ball thrown by the Calloways? That is almost laughable. If her gray garb covering every ounce of skin is any inclination of her financial status, then she'll have to work some sort of magic to ever set foot inside that particular party. I doubt very much that her magic is impressive, or I would have seen her in court. A woman like her, I would remember.

"That was not meant for another's eyes." She sneers, crossing her arms under her chest, emphasizing the curve of her breasts, and even as her lips twist with her distaste, she is still quite gorgeous. Possibly more so.

Folding the list back into a square, I chuckle under my breath. "It is quite lofty, this list."

"It is doable." Challenge shines in her gaze. A quiet determination burns within this woman and for a second, I am lost to it.

"Doable…" I lower the parchment to hand it back, and her fingers brush against it, only for me to yank it away. "With help."

"You are—"

"I am what?" Leaning forward, I find myself genuinely curious. The darkest parts of me demand to know.

"Words a lady should never speak aloud." Sonnet bites her lip now as if the edges of her teeth are the only things holding in her insults. Something twists low in my gut, something strange and needy. Something not entirely unpleasant.

"Go ahead. No one else is here to hear you say it," I whisper. When she shakes her head, I push again. "You know you want to."

Mostly I want to hear it. I want to know exactly what this woman thinks of me. It can't be worse than what I currently think of myself.

Then a slender finger jabs into my chest, hard enough to bruise. Good gods, her finger is like a dagger aimed straight at my heart. "You're a terrible, low-life, brute. A damn thief and cheat. An ass of a man who tries to steal from a woman and then taunts her. You may be handsome, Malcom Black, but your soul is as gray as ash."

Well, that was something. Of all the things I've been called before this is almost a compliment. My lips press into a straight line to conceal the laughter that wants to burst out of me. The crimson stain on her cheeks darkens and spreads to the top of her pointed ears.

"We've got to work on your insults. You really shouldn't pair them with a compliment." The words I say surprise even me. We? Since when did I decide that she and I are any sort of we? But the idea is there, an inkling of a plan already forming finally decided upon as her mouth parts in an 'O.' Yes, there could be a 'we' that benefits us both. "But I'm glad to know you think I'm handsome."

"I—"

A slow smirk spreads across my face.

"Your list has potential, and fortunately for you, you ran into me, and I'm the perfect man to help you with said list." My hand lowers enough that she is able to snatch the parchment out of my grip. She folds it once more and shoves it into her bag.

"Why would you help me?" Her eyes narrow, her knuckles turning white as she holds her bag tightly.

Is she going to hit me with it again? I can still

feel the heat in my face where the book inside had slapped me harder than I've been hit in quite some time. If this secretary work of hers falls through, she really does have a good shot at working something out as a boxer. I might even consider endorsing her if she ever decides to do so.

"A favor for a favor," I say, watching her hands. If I look up I might get snared in her eyes again.

Her grip loosens. "What sort of favor?" The skepticism in her features is clear.

I'll have to tread lightly, make my offer sound appealing. That can't be too hard. Most people trip over themselves to find themselves in my good graces. Could I be the one to tame such a raging woman?

This *must* be what rock bottom is.

If I hadn't gotten drunk and sloppy, letting my pride take control of me, I'd never have lost all that money. My father is right about one thing; I am an irresponsible jackass and am impressive only in the way that I am very talented at fucking up. This would be the final straw before I am cut off and cast out. Truly, I am desperate and this woman with her strength of will and ability to nearly knock a man out with a book might very well be my only saving grace.

Sonnet Weatherwood is my very own Yuletide gift sent straight from the holiday fates themselves. She just doesn't know it yet.

She'd said it herself. She could have robbed someone on this very path blindly without the charade I tried to pull. I mistakenly thought I might have the element of surprise on my side and that a woman might be so frightened she'd quake under my bulk and give in. I am in fact, clearly, an idiot. But she isn't...

"I'll help you complete that list of yours and you'll help me get back my gambling debt."

Sonnet takes a step back. Instantly, I miss the nearness of her and the heat, so similar to my own, that had radiated off her body as she'd grown more and more annoyed. Prowling forward, I refuse her the space.

"Absolutely not," she says with certainty. Another shot directed right at my heart. "I don't have any interest in bringing the man who tried to rob me as a date to any event much less kiss *you* under the mistletoe."

Another blush makes the harsh way she speaks soften. Is she imagining what it would be like to kiss me? The image flashes briefly through my mind though I try to shove it away without much success. If she kisses with as much passion and fervor as she speaks, then perhaps it wouldn't be so bad. I might even enjoy it. Then my own face grows suddenly hot.

Keep it together. Be persuasive, damn it.

With a wave of my hand through the air, I dismiss her notion altogether. "Of course not. I can help you find a date and someone else to kiss."

Though, would kissing me be so very bad? I sigh. I have been told on several occasions that I am quite good at it.

Her shoulders drop and something like disappointment flashes across her face before she hides it behind her mask of annoyance. It is quite the put-out look that she's giving me now.

Most women who attend the same events I appear at look at me with a sort of hunger, like I am something to be obtained and caught in the web their darling mothers are spinning about them. Normally, I am entertained by the notion even if I'm entirely not ready for marriage. It's nice to be wanted. Yet, Sonnet Weatherwood only looks like she is about a second away from knocking me out cold. And I firmly believe she'd try. Am I...into this?

"I have no money to give you," she continues.

"I don't expect you to pay me." She tilts her head in an unspoken question. *Right, Malcom, get to the point.* "I expect you to help me steal."

Both her brows rise under the sweep of black

fringe covering her forehead. Her full lips purse before she answers, "No."

"I'll give you time to think on it."

"No." She shakes her head now. "No. No. No. Definitely not. I can't. We can't. *I* am not a criminal."

"You're only a criminal if you get caught."

Once again, the damn woman is backing away, walking past me, as though I've been only a minor inconvenience on her way home. "I don't think that's how that works, Mr. Black."

My name rolls off her tongue and something like pleasure ripples down my spine.

"I'll start you off easy. Like a simple con or highway robbery." It's an effort to hide the amusement in my voice. One moment Sonnet was fighting me off like she a powerful lioness and now she's running away like some meek little deer at the thought of committing a crime. Truly, her innocence is admirable. Her moral compass might be made of gold. In which case, mine would be made of rusted iron. If I had one.

Perhaps I judged her wrong and she is indeed a goody-two-shoes who will run to the authorities and turn me in for this pathetic attempt at thievery. Then I'll be disowned and the laughingstock of the court.

"No," she repeats. Her tone is firm as she turns on her heal giving me her back.

"You can have the night to think on it."

The snow is slowing now, giving me a better view of her silhouette as she stomps away. A ravenous flower stretches into her path and she kicks the thing aside with the toe of her boot. Nothing and no one is getting in the way of that woman. Not one of the teeth-filled plants in the Bitten Woods and certainly not a down-on-his-luck son of a nobleman.

"My mind won't change!" she shouts back, voice echoing in the quiet of the night.

Mmm, we'll see about that.

"See you tomorrow, Poesy."

"It's Sonnet!"

"Whatever you say."

Standing in the center of the dirt path, I watch her leave. My heart does something nasty in my chest. An ache blooms in the center, so terrible, that I have to rub my palm against it.

My attempt at robbery didn't work but perhaps I have still been successful. Something tells me I'm far from done with Miss Weatherwood.

It's clear that Sonnet might be a hard sell, but she is smart as a whip and strong-willed enough to refuse me. Yes, she could very well be the answer to all my problems.

She's the only thing I think about on my long walk back home, then late into the night when I wake with the violent urge to ease my budding frustrations to the mental image of her sneer. I take myself in hand to the thought of her. Still, in my dreams, I cannot escape those brutal ocean eyes as though I am but a captain lost at sea.

I'll find a way to win her favor. Even if my next con is to trick her into it.

SONNET

Consciousness pulls at me like a fish ripped from the sea on the end of a fisherman's pole. Dreams of white-blond hair and a devilish smirk fade as my mattress dips and bounces. I blink and just like that the wicked gleam in those brown eyes is gone. My fog-filled mind tries to remember what I had been dreaming of and what is real for only a moment before my vision focuses on my sister's face.

Merry Weatherwood inherited our mother's whimsical nature and none of our father's seriousness. A wide smile splits her face and it's exactly what I might imagine our father's face could look like if he ever thought to grin.

"Go away." I grit the words through clenched teeth.

Though I wouldn't ever consider taking up boxing as Malcom might have suggested, had that been real and not a dream, there is one person I would consider boxing. My sister. Particularly when she's shaking my bed and waking me up.

"A package was just delivered for you." Merry reaches for the thinning quilts that keep what little warmth I managed to gather in and rips them away.

Brisk morning air washes over me. *Seriously*? Pushing my hair out of my face, I sit up and reach for the blankets giving her my best glare. Because, *rude*. Merry must be jesting to get me out of bed. The sun is only now stretching over the horizon and slowly pouring into my modest room. It certainly is too early for mail to be delivered.

"Leave me be. It was a late night." If my family thought to ask about it I'd blame it on a late evening at Dr. Lowen's office, but in reality, I'd laid myself down only to be caught in a violent storm of thoughts. Ridiculous, I know. Being the eldest daughter means stress and I are well acquainted, more so after last night's blunder.

Had Malcom Black really tried to rob me? Had the man truly thought to strike a deal with me? How badly do I really want that list to be completed? Very, unfortunately. Even the reminder of him reading said list turns my cheeks hot all over again.

Maybe I can pretend that last night never happened. The least I can do is try. Not that I am doing a good job at that. Already my mind replays the evening repeatedly. Damn that Malcom Black. I could, and should, turn him into the Court of Frost's guard. But would they even believe me? I hardly believe me. Plus, I don't need or want to start anything with the Black Family, especially before the holidays. Talk about counterproductive.

"I can't fathom waiting another second for you to open it. Please." Merry pouts, which she admittedly is quite good at. "Father has already made me wait an hour."

"An hour?! You've been awake for an hour already?" I scrunch my nose and frown. My entire house has always been earlier risers but with the work I'm doing now I can't make myself get out of bed any earlier than the sun is up.

My sister leans closer, whispering in my ear like she's confiding a secret. Her breath fans across my cheeks smelling like warm sugar. "Father made pancakes."

My stomach growls. Loudly. *Traitor*. I hadn't had time for dinner last night and I'd been far too exhausted and worried about waking my family to consider it when I'd finally arrived home.

"Fine. I'm up," I grumble and rub the sleep from my eyes, somehow managing not to wince at the chill as I set my bare feet upon the wooden floor. I can hardly open my eyes all the way, sleep still calling my name. My narrowed gaze makes my room fuzzy. The simple wooden dresser is only a brown blur next to my bed. The full-length mirror in the corner reflects the erratic strands of hair sticking off my head and my white sleeping gown.

Merry is already moving, her steps a patter through the house as she sprints away with a shrill cry of joy, and I follow along in exhausted silence. She's particularly energetic this morning——

With only one foot in the dining room, my steps come to a halt. The long wooden table, meant to seat fifteen and one of the few things we'd been allowed to take with us when we'd been forced to move after mother's death, holds a stack of fluffy pancakes on one side and a large white box on the other. My attention drifts over the box and the large black bow atop it. Tucked into the ribbon, a card waits with my name carefully scrolled across it.

I guess this isn't a joke and a means to get me out of bed early...

"A package for you!" Merry holds her arms

out dramatically showing off the rather obnoxious box. It's huge.

My father, Mr. Denver Weatherwood, sits perfectly straight at the head of the table, his brow arched, and a bit of pancake halfway to his mouth. "Do you have a suitor that I am not aware of?"

Nervous perspiration starts in my palms. I try to appease the terrible sensation by wiping my hands down the front of my billowing, white nightgown. "Absolutely not."

"Open it." Merry is squealing at this point, and I'd do anything to keep her from letting out any more of these atrocious shrill sounds at this ridiculous hour.

Damn all my good sense, I do desperately want to know what is in that box.

Exhaling I make my way to the table and work to remove the bow, gently enough that we might keep it and reuse it for our Yule gifts. My sister though, clearly loathing the pace I've set to open the box huffs a breath. The card slides free, and I make to open it only for Merry to hiss at me. Yes, hiss. Like a wild animal. Honestly, we should consider selling her to the zoo. Deadpanning in my sister's direction, I set the card aside and lift the lid.

Any air that had once been in my lungs is forcefully removed. My breath is stolen from me as I peer down at a glistening golden gown. Sparkling threads are intricately woven around the neckline and waist. Beads that catch the light like the warmth of the sun has been imbued within them lay against the bronze fabric. The dress shines like nothing I've ever seen before, like something made in the High Fae Courts that even the richest here in the Court of Frost hardly ever manage to get their hands on.

Merry gasps but the room stays otherwise silent as we look down at what could only be considered a piece of art. Even my father, who hardly seems impressed by much, stands from his seat and lets the pancake on the end of his fork slide off to fall back onto his plate with a *splat*. It takes several heartbeats for me to remember how my limbs work. When I am finally able to move again, I set down the lid and reach for the card. Turning over the envelope, a large black seal stares back at me, the letter B molded into its design. I break the seal. The weight of my family's gazes settle on my skin, stealing my focus so much so that I have to read the letter twice to understand what is inked across the page.

Miss Weatherwood,

I believe I owe you an apology. Though, crossing paths last night might be a sign from the gods that we should both heed. My apology comes in two parts. One fit for you this weekend and another for the younger sister I was not aware you had. I wonder if she's as ferocious as you are. Nevertheless, I hope you accept said apologies and come to join me for breakfast in Crecedence Corner.

Malcom

A bribe. I thought I'd lost my breath before but somehow there's more to expel. Malcom has gone a step further then gifting me the most gorgeous dress I've ever seen. He also gifted me a gown for my sister. *That* does manage to thaw part of my frozen aching heart. Damn, he's good. I hate him a little more for it too.

"Well, what does it say? Who is it from? You can't leave us waiting here like this!" Merry bounces and the dishes rattle on the table. The poor girl doesn't have a calm bone in her body.

"There is also a gift here for you." I watch her

from under my lashes as I lift the golden dress out of the box to reveal a second layer covered in yellow tissue paper. "The rest is for you."

Though I want to hold the dress away from me as if it is a disease I might catch, I can't help but revel in my sister's excitement as her jaw drops open.

"For me?" The question is hardly out of her mouth before the girl lunges forward and rips away the paper to reveal another gown underneath. The dresses themselves are quite the opposite. If mine is the sun then Merry's is the moon. It's as if a thousand stars have been spun into the dress though the neckline with an added bit of lace. "Tell me who sent this right now so that I might kiss them upon the mouth!"

"Merry Weatherwood you will do no such thing," our father rasps.

Still, the two of them stare at me waiting for an answer.

"I—surely, this was a mistake," I try to answer.

My sister glares and holds the gown to her body. "Hardly. This dress was made to fit me. Won't I look dazzling in it for Trudy's ball, Father?"

Father only stares at me waiting for a response. Merry is right though. These gowns came at the right time. We'd planned to wear one of our gowns from last season but we'd already been seen in them a couple of times now. These dresses are made to make the wearer stand out amongst a crowd. They'll be perfect to show the rest of the court that the Weatherwood sisters might have been knocked down but we certainly aren't out.

"Sonnet, who sent the dresses?" My father's voice is quiet and polite, but I know him well enough to know his patience is waning.

"Malcom Black."

"Malcom Black!" Merry screams.

Really, I can't blame my sister for that sort of reaction. After all, isn't that the same way I'd acted when I'd first seen him? His family is too prominent amongst the court to not know of him. And despite the last name Black, they all sport that brilliant white hair. A Black could not be missed. Their family is only second to the Calloways themselves.

"Why might Mr. Black be sending my daughters gowns?" Though his tone suggests a father's disapproval and concern, his eyes glisten with hope.

"He's invited me out for breakfast this morning." I set the gown down to hold up the card as proof. He waits in silence, somehow always knowing there is more, but I can't tell him that Malcom had tried to steal from me. He likely wouldn't believe me anyway. No one would. I'm not sure I even believe it, and it had happened to me! "We happened upon each other when I was leaving Dr. Lowen's office last night."

"Without a chaperone?" The color leaches from his face.

"I was still at the office. Dr Lowen was there." A lie. I swallow trying to rid myself of the lump in my throat. My falsehoods come too easily.

That appeases my father's distress and he nods a bit. "Well, you can't leave him waiting. I'll call Edmund around and dress to escort you—"

"No!" I say much louder than I mean to. "No, don't bother. Edmund can come in and chaperone."

"That's hardly his job." He frowns.

"It's just that I know that the cold bother's your back and I don't want to make anything worse on you. I'm sure Edmund won't mind." Not quite a lie but not quite the truth either. My hunger is quickly turning to nausea.

"Very well," he amends before shooing me off with a wave of his hand.

Leaving the gown and my sister, who's holding the dress to her body as she prances about the room, I hurry to change. Damn that Malcom Black for forcing my hand. I can't very well accept his gift and ignore his call to meet. Father would never allow me to cause such offense. The man clearly knows the games he plays and plays them well.

It's not long before I'm sitting inside my family's carriage swaying with the movement as Edmund drives me toward Credence Corner. I expect that when the carriage comes to a stop I'll find myself at a grand estate worthy of the Black name, but instead, we stop outside a quiet little café on the edge of Daydale. I stare at the plain wooden panels and the slightly crooked sign with the word 'Open' on the door.

Edmund pulls the door open, and I hold tightly to my cloak as I take his hand and step outside. Of all the servants we employed in our household before Mother's death, Edmund has been the only one who'd followed us to our new residence and accepted a much smaller salary in favor of staying with my family. He has a rather pointed face, a long nose with a bump in the center, and his pointed ears are visible through his short graying brown hair. The most notable thing about the man, though, is that his expression always holds a bit of kindness. I would be lying if I didn't say we'd all grown rather fond of him. So much so that he is more family than servant at this point.

"This is Credence Corner?" I ask, looking at the street sign and then over to the café once more. Through the windows, I can make out several full tables. People eating and laughing, all unaware that a thief is likely in their presence.

"Indeed." Edmund steps forward to escort me inside. "Shall I wait at the counter for you?"

The café is quite an adorable little space. A small fire is lit on one side of the room and fresh flowers are set about every table. I could have found the business itself to be cozy if it wasn't for the man seated in the back corner watching me with a predator's gaze. A shiver travels through me as I lock eyes with him.

I force my back straight and my chin high as I remove my cloak and hand it to Edmund. "Yes, please. Thank you, Edmund."

"Enjoy yourself, Miss Weatherwood," he responds before finding himself a seat along the counter amongst other single diners.

Gone is the dark clothing that Malcom had worn last night. Instead, he wears brown trousers and a loose cream-colored tunic that reveals a patch of white hair across the top of his chest. His sleeves are rolled up his forearms to reveal a silver chain upon his wrist. It shines with the fire-light as he stretches his arms across the back of his seat and waits for me to slide into the booth directly across from him.

"I expected you'd be in a better mood given the gift I sent over." His eyes trail over me as if he expected I'd come in the gown itself.

"Did you steal the dresses?" I intertwine my hands in my lap.

"Let's just say, I know a modiste who owed me a favor."

Great, now both me and my sister will be dressed in gowns from dubious origins.

"Sounds like quite the scandal."

Malcom snorts. "Hardly. My family and I are well versed in keeping that sort of thing quiet."

"And am I to be one of those things? I can't be bought with bribes, Mr. Black."

"No, I don't expect that you are." He leans forward, clasping his hands on the table between us. Even his long fingers sparkle with several rings. "That is why it was a gift and not a bribe. Nevertheless, I'll endeavor to keep this quick. I was serious about that deal I offered last night. I need someone small and smart to help me."

While I've always loathed my petite frame and height, men have always had some sort of fascination with it. As if they enjoy towering over women or keeping us hidden in their pockets.

"And in exchange," he continues, "I'll help you with that list of yours."

My entire body tenses at the mention of my list. I shouldn't have ever written it down and now that someone else knows about my goals, I've found myself quite embarrassed by them. As if I'm little more than a young teenager wishing upon a star.

"What list?" I feign ignorance.

"One. Make graceful reentry to society at Trudy's ball. Two. Get invited to Yuletide Ball. Three. Get a date to the Yuletide Ball. Four. Get kissed under the mistletoe—"

"Please. That is enough." I sigh with the urge to rub at the ache forming between my brows.

Though I am bothered by the idea of helping a man such as him, I can't help the nagging feeling in my gut. The part of me that screams at the chance to help my family back into good standing. The part of me that understands the eldest daughter's duties to find a man of wealth and good reputation to wed.

And all it would take is a small venture into the criminal world.

If word got out, the court gossips would eat this up, but I could do this one thing if it means getting everything I want for this holiday and setting my family up spectacularly for their future.

I thought heavily upon the deal for several hours of the night. Between dreams of Malcom's hands on my body and those full lips daringly close to mine, I'd imagined what my agreement in this matter could do for me.

"We will make a bargain," I demand.

"I thought you might say that." Malcom exhales the words as if he'd held his breath waiting for my response. From his pocket, he pulls a small knife, and though I know in theory that Fae bargains require blood, I've never stooped so low as to make one. To break a blood oath would mean one's immediate death, but to ensure that Malcom Black never speaks of this, I require it. So I hold out my hand.

To his credit, the man ignores the way I tremble as he cradles my hand and slides the blade across my palm. A slice of burning pain follows the knife. He repeats the act upon his own flesh and intertwines our fingers, his gaze holding steady upon mine. Heat encapsulates my hand.

"You will never speak of the crimes we commit. And you will tell no others of what my list entails," I whisper.

"You will assist me in my venture to regain the funds to cover my debt to my father, in whichever manner I find most agreeable," he adds.

How specific must one's deal be? I always hear that the details are important, so I continue, gripping his fingers tightly. By that logic that means he could turn me to the sheets of paying men, or the fighting cage of a bear if he wants to! *Absolutely not.*

"Be more specific," I grind out. "Nothing reprehensible or immoral."

"By means of theft." He tips his chin.

I cringe but keep going. I'm not happy with it but it can be done and still leave me with a shred of my morals left. "You will help me secure my invitation to the Yuletide Ball as well as secure me a date that might kiss me underneath the mistletoe." I pause a moment and add, "Said date cannot be yourself either."

He rolls his eyes. "You shall have no worries about me attempting to kiss you underneath any mistletoe."

Teeth digging into the inside of my lower lip, I nod. In our silence the cut along my palm prickles. When the sensation ends, Malcom drops my hand as if it's hot enough to burn him. I scowl and sit back in my seat.

"What now?" I sigh.

Returning the knife to his pocket, he pulls out another sealed envelope. "Take this. It details my plans. Read it. Memorize it. Burn it." He slides the letter forward with one finger.

Wow, he really is a storybook villain.

"This seems rather dramatic." I tuck the envelope away in my purse and pat it for good measure.

"We wouldn't want to harm your reputation

considering our bargain. It is a small but necessary precaution. You can read, can't you?"

You can read, can't you? I mock internally. What an ass.

I scoff. "Did you or did you not ask me to assist you because of my intelligence?"

"It was but a joke."

"Not one that I find remotely funny."

Malcom stands, straightens, and gives a slow smile that spreads across his face like butter melting across a hot pan. My heart flutters in my chest. His smile is little more than wicked delight. Perhaps in joining him on this venture, I am becoming a little bit wicked myself.

SONNET

My body jostles with the movement of the carriage as my family and I make our way through the streets of Daydale. Merry's shoulder brushes against mine and I only narrowly dodge her expressive hands as she prattles on about something. Her words somehow fill the space but are unable to truly penetrate my thoughts.

Today, I am thankful for my gloves as they cover my clammy palms. This is the moment I've longed for, the first event that will thrust my plans into action, and it's thanks to one, Mr. Malcom Black, that I do indeed look the part. Though, I'm not quite sure if I'm thankful or loathful. It is this gown, after all, that forced me to meet with him and ultimately accept this ridiculous plan. Still, it might be nice going in knowing I'll have more than Trudy to talk to. She'll be busy hosting anyway.

"You seem very contemplative, my dear." My father, Denver Weatherwood's, voice is the first to snap me to attention.

"She's probably dreaming about Malcom," Merry says, batting her lashes and pretending to swoon.

Gag me. Really, please, I'd rather be caught having a public episode of diarrhea than ever daydream and swoon over Malcom. Dreams of him are considered nightmares. And if I'm day dreaming about doing anything to him it's wringing his neck.

"Hardly," I snap, perhaps a bit too harshly, as Father gives me a knowing smile. I reach out to pat his hand and reassure him as much as myself that everything is fine. And nothing has to do with any real interest in Malcom Black.

It's. Fine. The only thing I'm interested in is having the best, most cheerful, holiday ever.

That's. It.

"A bit nervous. It has been so long since we've joined any of the court's festivities. I'm hoping we will be well received."

"As beautiful as my daughters are, I have no fear of that. If anything, I worry about you both being received too well. Magic or no."

Merry is still too young to be of marrying

age, but in the Court of Frost that never stops any man from looking. Suddenly, I have the urge to hide my sister in a cloth sack and make her hold my hand the entire time. Likely, Father feels the same as we pull up to the home of the Hollis Family and he begins to tug at his collar.

"I have no doubt this will go splendidly," I forcefully declare, not sure if I even believe myself.

Edmund pulls open the carriage door with a bow before offering his hand. The evening sun is nearly hidden by the massive estate. A sprawling brick building easily ten times the size of our current home. White shutters and flower boxes overflowing with poinsettias in bloom frame every large arching window. The white rock that leads us from the carriage and into the home appears as if each stone has been cleaned and polished to gleam underfoot.

I'd visited the Hollis' plenty of times before Mother's death, but I'd never truly seen the home or noticed its grandeur before. Now after being forced from my home, not too unlike this one, and into what I can only describe as a shack, I feel the wealth of this place deep in my bones.

Their shining tile floors and sweeping staircase leads to the ballroom already filling with bodies. Shimmering skirts and fanciful suits part and meet on the dance floor underneath a chandelier dripping in emeralds. Garlands are strung about the room, more poinsettias arranged in bursts of vibrant red along the strands. My gaze snags on the corner of the room as an eruption of giggles sound. A mistletoe hangs, waiting to induce romance as the couple that had stood below it scurries toward the dance floor.

Soon that will be me.

"Sonnet! You came!" Gertrude—Trudy—Hollis rushes toward me. There's a blur of red rubies and mouse-brown hair before I find myself wrapped tightly in a hug. Trudy's next words are muffled against my hair. A cloud of her sickly-sweet perfume surrounds me. "I wasn't sure if you'd still come seeing as you lost the king's favor once you lost your mother." Trudy's eyes are wide as she takes me in, holding me at arm's length. My chest squeezes tightly with the reminder of all I've lost and I'm happy for the space. Happier still that I have the new gown as she continues, "You look stunning! You can't even tell that your family lives in such a tiny modest home how."

The smile I force to my face is stiff. "That is a fact that I would like to keep quiet tonight if you don't mind."

Trudy, sshhhhh, I snarl internally.

"Of course, of course." Trudy, though, is already waving me off. "Mum's the word, am I right?" Then with a wink, she's off to welcome the next guest.

Well, that could have gone much worse, I suppose. At least she didn't shout about me being poor loud enough for the entire room to hear it.

"She's lively." My father sighs, guiding us to a quiet corner of the room. Trudy is his worst nightmare. Chatty. There is nothing he hates more than being trapped in polite conversation. Small talk has never been his strong suit.

I had only been to a few events when I was still considered a child and hadn't been allowed to participate in the activities offered. Though, it isn't unusual for the youngest in attendance to find a way to start their own circle for dancing far away from the actual dance floor. Before, I'd always admired the stunning beauty of a ball and longed to be a part of the romance that befell those couples who took to the music. Now, I still want those things, but they are tinged with anger. The splattering of red flowers across the room feels fitting when partnered with the knowledge that not one person, save for Trudy Hollis herself, had cared to speak to my family when we'd lost Mother. Does anyone here even remember us? Is our fairy court that shallow?

Bouncing on her toes, Merry busies herself, striking up a conversation with another young girl near us, but now, after looking forward to this day, I feel frozen. My quiet determination is stifled by the knowledge that these people care so little for us. Most of all, I realize, I want a friend. Though I know Trudy would humor me, there will be little time for her to attend to my nerves as she hosts.

For several long minutes, I stand beside my father who grabs two goblets of wine and offers me one. Our corner is starved for conversation as we sip our drinks and watch as more guests filter into the room. I nearly drink the entire contents of my cup when a prickling awareness settles over my skin. Eyes drawn straight to the source, I watch four heads of white-blond hair enter the room. If I didn't know better, I'd think them all siblings, but Mason Black and his wife, Charlotte Black, walk before their two boys. Malcom's brother, Eames, is practically his twin, just a younger version of the man I'd met out on that dirt road several nights ago.

No one of the family bothers to look in our direction, though I wonder if he can feel my stare on his back as I can't seem to pull my attention away. Malcom is a far cry from the black outfit of a thief or the loose linens of a man playing peasant. No, he's come in his finest clothes. A black tunic fitted to the muscular planes of his body is accented by a golden thread that weaves stars around his cuffs and collar.

He parts from his family with a kiss on his mother's cheek, and as the crowd notices him, the room in turn parts for him. How could anyone not notice Malcom Black? His family, with their power and wealth, is what everyone in the Court of Frost wants to be. Though none of them know Malcom's secret as I do.

It's that passing idea that makes me stand a little straighter. I hold the power here. I know what could destroy him. But I won't. Can't. Not if I want his help in achieving everything I need to get my family off on the right foot this Yuletide Season.

Malcom comes to a stop, shaking hands with a man I quickly recognize as Cassius Calloway. The eldest son of the family that hosts the largest event, the Yuletide Ball, that I'm so desperate to get an invitation to. My mouth goes dry. How had I not seen that Cassius was already here?

As though he finally notices me watching, Malcom's brown eyes lock with mine over Cassius' shoulder. I force a breath as his attention trails the length of my body before settling on my face again.

Being a wallflower has its benefits as I doubt anyone is paying me much attention when I mouth, '*invite me over*' to Malcom. He blinks at me. I sigh and try again with, '*introduce us.*'

"If you wish to speak with someone," my father whispers, "it is best to do so with sound."

I send him a scowl before turning my glare back to Malcom. His brows are bunched together now, clear confusion written all over his stoic features. I try my best to mime the meaning of my words to him, slowing the movement of my lips as I repeat, '*introduce us.*'

'*What*?' he mouths back.

My palm has the sudden urge to meet with my forehead. How can one man be so beautiful and so stupid at the same time?

'*Introduce us.*' Father snorts as I frantically motion between myself and Cassius Calloway.

Malcom's lack of attention is enough for Cassius himself to finally turn to follow his friend's gaze all the way back to me. My entire body goes stiff, and I look away with a tight smile. Heat quickly gathers in my cheeks.

Well, this can't be going any worse.

Then Malcom is parting from Cassius and striding up to me with a look of annoyance.

I was wrong. It can totally get worse.

With my gloved fingers, I pinch the bridge of my nose when he stops before me, giving Father a nod of respect. "Mr. Weatherwood. Miss Weatherwood." He reaches for my hand, plucking it from massaging my brows, and brings my fingers to his lips. He looks up at me through his white lashes, his dark gaze spearing straight through me. My stomach knots several times over as I swallow to try and ease the dryness of my throat.

Thief. Liar. Wicked. I remind myself.

"Mr. Black." My father bows. "I'll be"—he glances at me—"right over there." Then he strides several feet away leaving us somewhat alone but certainly watched.

I rip my hand from his and he smirks down at me. "Is something wrong with you?"

"Is something wrong with me?" I want to clutch my chest but force my arms to my sides. "What is wrong with *you*?"

"I was not the one making uniquely weird facial expressions and tossing my hands about as though I was conducting an orchestra."

"I—" I grit my teeth. "Cassius' family hosts the Yuletide Ball."

"I am aware." His hands find his pockets and he looks down at me as though bored by our conversation.

"And said ball is the one I wish to attend."

He nods.

"Introduce. Us."

His eyes narrow. "Is that what you were getting at?"

"Yes!"

"Well, by all means," he holds out his arm for me to take, "let me introduce you."

If I rolled my eyes any harder, they might get stuck in the back of my skull. Still, I slip my hand into the crook of his elbow, keenly aware of his warmth through our clothing. Only once do I offer a glance back at my father, who has decided to busy himself studying the floral arrangements, and my sister, who already started a small circle for the youngest of them to dance in.

It is while we walk arm in arm to Cassius and the small group with whom he converses that I notice several pairs of eyes on us. Even Trudy stops speaking to one of her guests to watch us.

"Is it always like this?" I whisper.

"Like what?"

"People watching you everywhere you go."

Malcom hums quietly. "You get used to it."

How might I get used to this? I'm suddenly the object of so many people's attention I can hardly figure out what to do with myself. There isn't time for me to compose myself in front of the crowd before we stop before Cassius Calloway.

The man, though beautiful at a distance, is somehow more stunning up close. Golden curls are brushed away from his face, eyes as blue as the ocean are flecked with silver, and I'm certain his jaw could cut through diamond.

"Cassius, might I introduce Miss Sonnet Weatherwood." Malcom smiles politely, casually dropping my arm, before he does a doubletake and whispers. "You can close your mouth now."

Oh no. I was in fact gaping. Snapping my jaw closed, I smile before giving him a practiced curtsey.

Cassius looks from me to the group briefly before smiling back. "Malcom, you dirty dog, is this the beauty who grabbed your attention?"

Malcom's smile falters. "Miss Weatherwood and I have recently become acquainted."

Ugh, and the way he says it sounds as though it's painful for him to even announce.

"Well, if he isn't going to appreciate such a fine creature as yourself, then I certainly must." Cassius sets aside the wine in his hand and turns to face me fully. I lift my head to look up at the man who easily towers over the group. "Miss Weatherwood, might I have this dance?" He offers his arm.

"Please, call me Sonnet." I settle my hand on his arm. This is a dream come true! Dancing, with Cassius?! A couple of bumps along the way but tonight might work out in my favor.

It's a wonder that I remember how to walk much less dance as Cassius leads me out onto the dance floor. I swear I hear my sister's squeal but politely ignore it as the music starts and we turn to face each other. His fingers grasp mine and an arm loops around my waist pulling me close. More heat gathers in my cheeks at our nearness.

"I've not seen you in court. Are you new to the area? I'm certain I would have remembered a face as striking as yours." Cassius' voice is low and vibrates against my ear.

"I had only recently come of age when my mother passed away. We've been away for several months, mourning."

When I inhale, my chest brushes against his, and the desire to settle my head on his shoulder rises like a tidal wave within me. Though I ignore it and think to compare the space between us to the others around us to ensure that we remain at a proper distance. We are close but we aren't closer than any other couple on the floor.

"My condolences." He dips his chin and I catch wind of his strong aftershave. "I am lucky, though, that you've found a friendship with Malcom so that I might be acquainted with you now."

"I may be the lucky one." I can't help but beam up at him. What a gentleman.

His smile is blindingly brilliant, and my heart begins to gallop in my chest. He spins me in time with the music and I swear he pulls me a fraction closer when I return to his arms.

"I will be seeing you more this season, I hope?"

"I—"

A hand curls over Cassius' shoulder, stopping our dance short.

"Might I cut in?" Malcom's voice greets my ears before his eyes, cast in a new sort of darkness, reach mine.

MALCOM

5

Staring down at the glittering gold threads circling my cuffs, I pretend to pick at a loose one. Anything is better than watching Cassius and Sonnet spinning about the dance floor. Others carry on some semblance of a conversation around me, but the words feel muffled against the pounding of blood in my ears.

The modiste truly outdid herself. Both Weatherwood girls are the shining stars of the Hollis' ballroom. Or, in Sonnet's case, the sun. The entire room watches her out on the dance floor, some knowing who she is, others curious as to where she came from. None of them realize that somehow Sonnet is the center from which the event now moves.

I know, and I had known the moment I

walked through the doors. I'd seen the gowns of gold and silver from the corner of my eyes and forced myself not to look her way. If I had, I'd have walked straight to her and that would have only caused the court to whisper. I don't need anyone whispering more about me than they already do. Then, when I locked eyes with her, I suddenly forgot myself. I'd been too interested in her beauty to even fathom what she'd been trying to say to me. In short, I'm an idiot. A lustful, shallow, idiot.

What have I gotten myself into? Perhaps this deal will turn sour and I'll still be ruined and disowned by my father.

An elbow nudges my side. "Malcom."

Glancing up, I blink several times, trying to force myself into reality. "Hmm?"

"I'm surprised you allowed Cassius to sweep her off to the dance floor. One might think you'd have asked her yourself." Marcus Delroy, son of the owner of the most profitable gentlemen's club in Daydale, gives me a sly smile.

"Miss Weatherwood and I are nothing more than friends. If Cassius should want her I see no reason to stop his pursuit." But the words feel wrong leaving my lips. A simmering annoyance begins in the pits of my stomach as I watch them head off arm in arm.

"Then perhaps I will ask next, especially if

she has no qualms being held so close," Thomas Jameson, who claims to be a distant cousin of the King himself and with enough money to back up the statement, snickers.

My attention snaps back to the dance floor. Indeed, as the music picks up and women are twirled and brought back to their partners, Cassius has Sonnet held with so little room between them, I wonder if so much as a strand of hair could fit in that space. The stirring of annoyance warms to something like anger. Before I can stop myself, I'm across the dance floor, hand reaching for Cassius' shoulder.

None of this is proper or how one ought to act. In fact, cutting in on their dance is seen as quite rude. Yet, I decided in the half a heartbeat between my spot on the edge of the dance floor and here that I would rather be seen as rude than risk her reputation. I'm not known for being proper anyway.

"Might I cut in?" No sooner have the words left my mouth than Sonnet looks up at me with those wide brilliant blue eyes narrowed.

The smile falls from Cassius' face, a look of question in his gaze that I ignore, but for Cassius to refuse would only make this situation a thousand times worse and I know the man will find little reason to fight for Sonnet, whom he hardly knows. So with a gracious bow, Cassius leaves the dance floor and returns to the group of men who watch with rapt interest. I finally let loose a held breath.

Now that I'm here, I can hardly bring myself to look down at her. Her attention sears my skin as I gently take her hand and hold her at an appropriate distance away from my body. Though some small portion of me begs and pleads to ignore social propriety and bring her closer than even Cassius had.

"Why did you do that?" Her polite smile masks her fury but it can't hide the bite of her tone.

"I know you think me impolite, but I am merely protecting your reputation. The Calloways hardly invite women whom they have sampled and tossed aside to the Yuletide Ball."

She stiffens in my arms.

I'm messing this up. Saying all the wrong things. That's not what I mean. Or at least not how it's supposed to come out.

"Are you insinuating that I'm some sort of harlot?"

I have to glance at her face and force myself to memorize her anger. "I—no." I exhale slowly. "Cassius isn't known for his kindness. What you might take as flirtation now he will surely use to mock you later. I'll help you get to that Yuletide Ball but I'll not let him ruin you in the process."

As swiftly as the song had started the music begins to fade and transition to something slower. I stop our movement, pull away, and watch her. Tension riddles her jaw, muscles clenching in an odd sort of contrast to her delicate features. Those blue eyes burn with rancor.

"It is quite interesting to hear you warn me off of someone when I know for a fact how wicked *you* are."

Something in my chest tightens, perhaps even cracks, like a spear of ice has been shoved into my heart. My fury is not far behind it though to soothe over the cold ache with its torturous heat.

"You have yet to see my wicked side." I smirk. "And though I would love to show you, it would be improper to do so outside of the bedroom."

Her attention stays on mine as she dips into a curtsey. Still, I relish the way her face turns a beautiful shade of red. It doesn't take much more than that to picture her flushed and sweating above me, riding my body through waves of pleasure. Fuck. I grit my teeth forcing the image away. We are to use each other and both be on our separate ways after and nothing more.

"Now, if you'll excuse me, Poesy," I whisper, "I shall be off to show your sister my wicked ways." I turn toward the place I'd seen her playing amongst the other younglings only to be stopped by Sonnet's fingers digging into my elbow and pulling me to a stop with quite impressive strength.

"You'll do no such thing with her."

Oh, there is fury in those words. A strong, almost motherly, possessiveness that tells of the wild thrashing beast that might live within this poised and proper lady. I want to see her unleashed.

Forcing a smile to my face, knowing all eyes are still on us, I give her hand a little pat. Only then does she realize that we are still very much on the dance floor and her features soften.

"Relax, wild thing, I'm only going to ask her to dance. It will look well to have your family joining in the festivities so that you might acquire future *invitations*."

Then her hand is gone but I can still feel the pressure of her touch. Still, I wonder what it might be like to feel that touch wander and explore the expanse of my body.

Damn it.

I'm staring at her. And she at me. Neither of us moving.

A heartbeat passes and another.

"Thank you," Sonnet says before strolling casually off the dance floor.

Internally, I curse again, because all I can do is stand here and watch as she walks away.

Sonnet

My body is warm. Why am I so warm??

I haven't begun to sweat but I'm pulling at the neckline of my dress and fidgeting with my sleeves trying to relieve the swell of heat that has overtaken my body.

Surely, it's all my nerves. Being back in court now feels as though I'm playing a game I've never been taught the rules for. Or perhaps I'd once been taught the rules but they've suddenly been changed.

"A dance with Cassius Calloway and Malcom Black all in one night," a voice sings over my shoulder. Sucking in a breath, I turn to see Trudy watching me with a feline smile. "Two of Daydale's most eligible bachelors. The way Malcom charged out there and interrupted that dance I have to wonder if he is smitten. Actually, it's not just me wondering." One of her gloved hands gestures about the room.

My attention glides over the room, snagging on more than one pair of watchful eyes. Men who look at me as if I'm a curiosity and women who both smile and glare over their wine glasses.

This is what I wanted, right?

"No, not smitten." *More like endlessly annoyed*. "Just newly acquainted. He was doing me a favor to introduce me since he was aware of my nerves about attending."

"Interesting." She practically purrs the word. "I've never known Malcom to be kind to anyone. He prefers his women much like he prefers his prey while hunting—with claws. Do you have claws, Sonnet?"

Claws. Like a wild animal.

Wild thing, he'd called me.

I don't have another moment to consider the notion before Trudy tips back with a boisterous laugh. "I'm joking of course." She pats my shoulder and lowers her voice to a hush. "I've only come to ask if you'd like to stay for the after party."

"After party?" I blink.

Somehow, Trudy's grin lifts further, her eyes twinkling with a terrible mischief. "A private party. If your father asks, yes, there will be chaperones," she says while also shaking her head no. My brows pull low. Court is to be immensely confusing if people will constantly be saying one thing and meaning another. "I'm inviting Malcom and Cassius and they might be more inclined to join if you're also coming. Plus, you're my friend and I do wish you'd stay."

Across the dance floor, Malcom has Merry held at a respectable distance hurrying her about at a comical rate. One that Merry clearly enjoys as she giggles and plays along. This man who beams at my little sister as though they are long-time friends is at such odds with the one I met in the Bitten Woods. I'm not quite sure what to do with the two sides of him.

"Tell me you'll stay." Trudy tugs on my arm now.

"Of course, I would love to. I'll confirm with my father but I'm sure it will be no problem. Especially if there will be chaperones." I give a wink though my stomach twists with the thought of lying to my father.

I must do my part to secure an advantageous marriage. And I'll do whatever I must to make sure this is the best Yuletide yet.

SONNET

It takes a moment for my eyes to adjust to the dim lighting of one of Trudy Hollis' sitting rooms. The heat of the overly crowded ballroom is gone but is replaced by the stuffy warmth of a large fire. With half a mind to strip off my gloves, I move through the people, most of whom I only know by name, and stop when I reach the window. Fog already covers the glass I so badly want to press myself against for relief.

Someone cheers when they find an iced bottle of brandy. How can one drink so very much? I've only had a few glasses of wine and already my body feels impossibly light, like one strong breeze might blow me away.

Pulling my gaze away from the window, I allow my attention to sweep over the room and the people.

The Hollis family already dressed their home for Yule. Even this private space has garlands strung across the mantle and above the arching windows. Shining silver and gold trinkets shaped like wrapped boxes sparkle across every available surface of the coffee tables and bookshelves. An evergreen tree is propped in the corner strung up with tinsel and red baubles on every branch. It would warm my heart if it didn't make me so unbelievably jealous.

I haven't gotten my family a tree for Yule yet. We'll need something, I suppose, to keep our gifts under. Perhaps I'll add it to my list and make Malcom chop one down and lug it into my house. That would be a sight to see! Still, I have to repress the shudder of repulsion as I think about Malcom setting foot inside our modest home that lacks all the riches and marvels that his certainly has.

No. I'll have to get a tree myself.

"A drink?" a deep voice asks from over my shoulder, as an arm reaches around and cages me in against a tall, sturdy body to offer me a glass of amber liquid.

My face heats further as I stare up into Cassius Calloway's striking blue eyes. *Don't panic, Sonnet. He's just like anybody else.* "I—" I smile down at my hands, clearly panicking. No part of me truly wants to drink. The way my body feels not quite my own is already so disarming, but it's Cassius...and to turn down a drink from the man with the most powerful family in court...that would be unfathomable. So I nod once and accept the drink.

His arms stay near me for a heartbeat longer before he straightens, his gaze trailing down my body. I feel his attention as it rakes down my body.

"I am pleased to see that you've stayed. You must be in the habit of keeping good company." There's a pleasant ring to his voice, one that sends goosebumps down my arms.

Sipping my drink, I refuse to allow myself to crinkle my nose at the bitter burning taste and force down a swallow. "I'm ever so grateful to have been invited." I pause long enough to catch his gaze. "And I only keep the very best of company."

A snort comes from somewhere over my shoulder, though I don't have to look to know who it came from. Still, the owner can't help himself, he's quite used to being the center of attention, I muse.

"Come now, Cassius." Malcom nudges his friend's shoulder, making the liquid in his cup slosh and threaten to spill out onto my gown. I shoot him a warning glare that I quickly mask with a smile when Cassius looks my way. "We both know that we are truly rotten company."

"Downright devilish," says a woman I don't recognize as she curls against Malcom's tall frame.

Annoyance shoots through me, though it's surely only because she's insinuating something about Cassius. I watch Cassius' face carefully, wondering if perhaps he likes the playful insults.

He steadies his drink and one half of his mouth lifts. "Speak for yourselves, I've got an honorable reputation to uphold."

"Right." Malcom scoffs, circling his arm around the woman's waist and walking toward the arrangement of furniture. Though I note his eyes linger on Cassius and me. Even when he fully turns away he never as much as glances at the girl by his side.

I pity the woman I already decided not to like. To be wrapped up in Malcom's arms but never get his full attention...he doesn't spend a lick of his charm on her. How unfortunate.

"Do not listen to him," Cassius whispers, leaning close enough for his breath to blow across my cheek. He smells of liquor and that sickly sweet cologne that clings to his clothes. "We are not as bad as he might make us out to be."

"I know better than to believe Malcom's

drunken ramblings." I know better than to trust him much at all. Yet, I'd somehow found myself in a bargain with him. Thankfully, we're both bound by the oath so I don't so much need to trust him as I trust the magic that holds us to keep him true to his word.

"Mmm," he hums, his eyes doing that trailing thing again that leaves me swaying on my feet. "Oh, look, it's snowing." His arm stretches across me to point out the window at the drifting flakes that float down to gather finely on the rooftop.

"Oh, how lovely!" It could be the drinks flowing through my blood or it could be that the Hollis' yard is quite picturesque—a long curving driveway, an open green yard framed by ever-green trees, and fat snowflakes falling to blanket it all in white.

Then fingers gently brushing along my chin turn my face back toward Cassius. "Not as lovely as the woman standing in front of me though."

What a line. I love it. Yes, say more things like that to me.

He's there. A breath away from me, lips so close all I need to do is tilt my head. My heartbeat stutters in my chest. *Wait—am I even breathing?* I force myself to inhale and Cassius' sly smile grows.

I caution a glance at the rest of the room. The

men are drinking more heavily now. Women leaning into them and giggling. But no one is as close as Cassius and I. I want to be closer still.

This is what I want. His attention. It's the best way to get my invitation and possibly even a date. My smile feels wrong on my face as I arrange my features into something demure and even a little bit flirtatious.

"Love birds!" Trudy's voice interrupts, saving me from whatever potentially might have come next. Cassius' smile falls a little but he turns to look at our host. "Come sit. We're playing a game."

"A game?" I ask, hopeful.

This might help break the ice and get me into the good graces of those in attendance tonight. More than Cassius and Malcom. The latter arranges himself on the arm of the couch, his body stretching to lean against the back, practically draping himself over the woman. He watches me and Cassius join the group with hooded eyes, his cheeks flushed. I have half a mind to stick my tongue out at him, but instead, I let my attention drift over him as though I hadn't noticed his attention. Even though I always feel his gaze on me.

"Truth or dare!" Trudy squeals.

I blink. Force another smile. Take a purposeful sip of my drink.

"Hmmm," Trudy says, tapping a finger against her lips. "Who should go first?"

There's an array of answers, of men and women nudging each other in hopes of volunteering their friends. Trudy turns in a slow circle looking around the small crowd with narrowed, assessing, and mischievous eyes. Only when Trudy stops, her attention directed at me, do I notice Cassius has his arm raised and a finger pointed at me. I look at him only for him to hide his hand behind his back with a wink.

"Sonnet!! Yes, since you're finally out of mourning I think you should start us off. What a wonderful idea, Cassius." Trudy beams up at the man before clapping her hands. "Truth or dare?"

This isn't a life or death question, but for some reason, my body is unaware of that little fact. Sweat builds along my spine. My heart hammers. And everyone is watching me, waiting for an answer.

Truth... could have me announcing something I don't wish to share. And there are *plenty* of things I don't want anyone in this room to know about me. None of these people need to know where I live, or that I have no magic, and they certainly don't need to know how Malcom and I met.

Dare... what if they ask me to kiss someone?

Or show them a glimpse of the magic I don't have?

Both answers can provide ample opportunity to embarrass me. Or ruin me.

"Dare," I answer on an exhale. *Does this make me a glutton for punishment?*

Several people in the room cheer and Cassius gives me an encouraging pat on the back.

I can do this. No matter what it is. I'll figure it out.

Trudy taps her finger against her lips again. "First dare of the night. It has to be something good. We'll save the juicy stuff like stolen kisses for later." She winks and I swear I hear Cassius groan in defeat behind me. I know it should thrill me that he's already thinking of stolen kisses but all I feel is relief and a pressure taken off my shoulders for the moment.

"She could steal something," one of the other women offers.

Trudy's green eyes go wide. "Yes! That's perfect." She claps again. "Sneak into my father's office and bring back evidence."

Thievery? Are all of Malcom's friends some shade of criminals? What on earth have I gotten myself into? I try my best to swallow back my anxiety.

"Where is your father's office?" I ask, my voice thankfully holding firm.

"Just down the hall. But it is locked. Unless you know how to get past the wards on the door. You could crawl out on the roof and in the window, I suppose. I've gone in a few times myself this way." She shrugs earning several bouts of giggles from her own admission.

"It's snowing. That's too dangerous. It's too slick." Malcom rolls his eyes.

"There's no way she'll accept that." Another voice chimes in.

And another. "Too risky."

"*She* couldn't do that." One last voice.

But Trudy only waves their concerns off. "Let the girl decide for herself. Sonnet Weatherwood, do you accept your dare?"

The woman at Malcom's side frowns a little as he sits himself up fully. His watchful eyes holding me hostage.

Behind me, Cassius whispers, "You can do this."

I don't want to disappoint him... or anyone else in this room for that matter. What choice do I really have? After all, it's only just begun to snow; the roof can't be too slick. If I can walk through the Bitten Woods alone I can crawl across and roof and into Trudy's father's office and snatch something. Easy. Sssooo easy, I try to convince myself.

"I accept."

The room cheers. Several glasses clink together.

Malcom stands abruptly.

Before I can let my fear get the better of me, I hand Cassius my drink and head straight for the window I'd previously occupied. Where I once stood and my breath had fogged the glass has since turned to frost. Cold radiates from the glass pane, raising goosebumps along my arms. I curl my fingers around the frame, the rough grain of the wood prickling against my palms. Inhaling, the thudding beat of my heart momentarily drowns out the excited chatter of the room, and I lift the window.

A pale hand slaps against the glass, keeping the window from opening more than a fraction. "You don't have to do this," Malcom whispers. Blond hair as white as the snow falls over his forehead as he leans closer. "The entire roof is a sheet of ice."

But there across the way is Cassius, grinning ear to ear, and watching with keen interest. He'd practically signed me up for this dare, though I didn't truly wish to be crossing an icy roof ever in my lifetime. The voice in the back of my head croons, reminding me of my duties as the first daughter and the dire need to establish my family in court once more. If I cannot gain a foothold with magic then I'll do it by pure will.

I lift my chin and hold Malcom's gaze as I keep my voice soft and low. "Consider this practice for when we call in that bargain."

A muscle along his jaw ticks, but he straightens and waves a hand at the window. "Be my guest. But there will be no deal if you fall and break your neck."

"Do try and have some faith in me."

He scoffs. "I tried to warn you, Poesy. Go if you must, but I will not be watching as you fall and break your pretty little neck."

The malice in his voice sends a thrill down my spine. I smile up at him and grin wider still as I see a flash of something in this dark gaze. The window groans in protest as I push it the rest of the way up and someone shouts with glee behind me. Their amusement at my potential suffering has me wondering about the types of people I'm currently surrounded by. Wicked ones, I think.

The wind whips through the room, pulling strands of my hair out around my face. Without my coat, I can already feel the frigid air settling into my bones. I clench my jaw to keep my teeth from chattering. Bodies shift closer to me now, my peers all coming to stand around the window, ready and eager to watch me either succeed or embarrass myself. Thus, making me tonight's entertainment. Perhaps one day, I'll look back at this and wonder how the hell I got into this predicament. Not today. I can't think too long or hard about this. But one day.

My hands tremble only for a moment before I gather the front of my skirts and hike myself up into the window frame. Snow soaks into the gown, wetting me down to my stockings.

"You've got this, Sonnet," Trudy whisper-shouts with a pump of a fist.

I only let myself catch a glance of my friend's smile before I plant my hands in the snow on the roof and push myself up to stand. The window, the one that would lead into Mr. Hollis' study, can't be more than twenty feet away. Dark-stained wood surrounds the peak of the dormer. Moonlight sparkles in the glass panes.

Twenty feet. I can make it twenty feet. I will make it. It's simple. One foot in front of the other.

Evergreen branches scratch at the side of the building and the wind howls as it picks up speed. From the rooftop of the Hollis' residence, every-thing else is so small. Even the people who stick their heads out the window behind me to watch feel as if they are miles away as I take one step and then another.

Each time I place my foot down before me, snow and ice crunch before I feel my foot slide ever so slightly. Inhaling, cold stabs at the back of my throat. Sweat builds and turns to ice against my skin. Then my foot slides out from underneath me, and my knee hits the rooftop with an audible *thwump*. Ice bruises my hands as I catch myself and my heart lurches into my throat. Okay, so maybe one foot in front of the other isn't the best plan. Behind me, there is a chorus of yelps and sighs of relief, maybe even a couple of sets of giggles. They are like my own cheering squad but I'm not sure if they are rooting for me to make it or to fall...

I'm nearly halfway across the roof, and I'm not going to look back at them. I try to force my feet underneath myself again only to crash back onto my knees. *Ouch. New plan.* Grinding my teeth, I set forth on my hands and knees. The flesh on my palms quickly goes from uncomfortable to burning to nearly numb as I reach the other window and fumble to take hold of it before lifting it with a grunt.

The study is dark, with only one light creeping in coming from under the door and the moon behind me. The other room is clapping, someone is chanting my name. All the noise vibrates through the walls of the home. Malcom was wrong. This isn't too dangerous for me and I'm about to impress the stockings right off everyone in the next room over. Everything is going as planned, and I'm going to secure my invite to the Yuletide Ball.

Snow melts off my heels as I go feet-first into the room. My eyes slowly adjust to the dim lighting and I can make out the rough shape of a chair, the desk before it, shelves on one side of the room, and a small sitting area past that.

I need to take something back with me. A book? No that would be much too heavy and large to bring back. His quill? I'd hate to end up with ink on this gown or ruin a perfectly fine quill. I come to stand next to the desk, scanning the piles of paper and the pots of ink. Moonlight glints off a green gem holding down a stack of correspondence. With an exhaled laugh, I snatch it up and weigh it in my hand. It's small enough that I can easily palm it, but it doesn't weigh enough to make it cumbersome. Perfect. This little paperweight is perfect, indeed.

Smiling to myself, I sit on the windowsill and swing my feet around. I've made it this far, all I have to do is get back across the roof. The back of my heels dig lines into the snow as I slide down enough to close the window behind me. Someone is cheering my name again and another person gasps from the windowsill as I turn myself back toward them. Every print I'd made in the snow has already iced over, which I learn far too quickly as I place my foot in one and immediately slip.

Cursing under my breath, I slide several

inches before managing to come to a stop. Perhaps I'll have to go the full twenty feet on my hands and knees again. Safer that way, after all.

On my hands and knees, I crawl across the roof to the peering eyes and smiling partygoers; the paperweight feels odd in my hand as I put weight onto it.

Trudy's hands are clasped in front of her face as if in prayer. Nowhere is there a glimpse of Malcom's white hair or pretty brown eyes. It is only me, the most prominent heirs of the court, and the green paperweight held tightly between my fingers. I fight a shiver as an icy current of air curls around my body. My fingertips, while gloved, are going numb but I force myself the last few feet. The windowpanes are pushed as far out as they can go to fit as many curious faces as possible to watch me.

I reach with my free hand, fingers grazing against the old wood. A skittering of ice tumbles from the roof's edge, crashing somewhere in the yard. I push my weight into the toe of one heel. Snow shifts underfoot. My leg slides. Arms wheeling for something to grab, only an inch away from the window, ice and snow give under my weight.

And I begin to fall.

Malcom

The worn wood of the windowsill bites against my hips, the only thing anchoring me inside the Hollis' home. Wide blue eyes framed with thick dark lashes stare up at me as though I'm her only hope. It's a stare that goes beyond my flesh and blood and dares to take a look at the writhing black thing inside of me that I call a soul. For a moment, I wonder if Sonnet can see the wounds I try so hard to hide.

Golden silk gloves, purchased from my own failing fortunes, threaten to slide right out of my grip. I curl my fingers harder around her arm. My nails dig into the expensive cloth. I'll be damned if this woman falls from this roof to her death. She's only here, at this party, taking this damn dare because I made sure she was. I need her. I need her to help me with one last job. Sonnet Weatherwood, while in the hands of the greedy, ambitious, heirs of the Court of Frost is my responsibility.

"My glove," she whimpers, her heels scrambling against the icy shingles. A small green stone is held in her other hand, dangling uselessly at her side. "Don't let me go," she pleads even as I feel her arm slip further from my grasp, sliding from her glove.

"Give me your other hand." The words come through my grinding teeth. It's truly a wonder I haven't chipped a tooth at this point.

"Oh no, oh no, oh no," someone, likely Trudy, says quietly behind me. Yet I don't see anyone else dangling out this window to help. *Fucking fools.*

Sonnet glances down at her hand, the prize she's worked so hard to get, and then back up at me. "Poesy, let the *damn* thing go and *give me* your other hand."

"I—"

Her hand slides free of her glove. Her heels smack against the roof, digging into snow and thick layers of ice. She screams and the sound bounces around my skull, clawing into my brain, my very being, as if she's digging her nails into my very person.

Shit.

I lunge, stretching dangerously into the space that separates us, my other hand, meeting the flesh of her fingertips. The brilliant red of her fingers is a stark contrast to the white of my skin. She must be freezing out there. I let her glove slip from my grip to fasten both hands on her. And I pull. Sonnet isn't heavy; such a petite thing like her is nothing once I'm able to get a solid hold of her. Her weight collides with my chest and I don't have the sense to let her go, to stop pulling her to me as if she is the only thing that might save me. She *is* the only thing that might save me.

The press of her body molds every curve of her figure against me. Her softness topples against me and the two of us stumble back into the onlookers. Air is pushed from my lungs as I land against the floorboards and Sonnet lands on top of me. An elbow manages to work its way into my ribs and I grimace.

Cold radiates off of her, making every part of our bodies that touch that much more notice-able. My hands are still wrapped around her, what warmth I can offer quickly heating her skin and working her already wind-kissed cheeks into a deeper, prettier, shade of red. Seconds pass that I hold her gaze. The swift relief of having her is taken from me as reality comes crashing back down. The room is a mixture of cheering and questions being launched at Sonnet. She breaks the steady look between us to smile up at Cassius who's come to squat somewhere near my head. He offers his hand.

My upper lip curls as she pulls her gloveless hand from mine and lets it settle into his grip. Our deal is the only thing tying us together. She's not here for me. She's a tool to be used. I try to remind myself of these things and force my lips together to suppress the growl that wants to work its way up my throat. She's here for Cassius. Sonnet is a smart girl and she's doing what she needs to do for her family. So, why do I feel like I might hurl my guts up all over the Hollis' expensive rug as she stands at Cassius' side and holds up the gem?

I'm always second to Cassius fucking Calloway.

Everyone screams in triumph. Arms shoot into the air, fists raised in excitement. She certainly is the star of this evening. It's all but confirmed when I finally stand and catch the way Cassius watches her. I'm all too familiar with what that haughty smile means and the way his attention drifts over her body as if he's already imagining her naked. Cassius isn't dumb. He knows Sonnet is in a position to want what he can give her, though she doesn't strike me as the type of woman willing to fall into his bed. No, she has much more self-respect than that.

Still, the urge to shove him away from her lingers.

"You've done it!" Cassius hollers, sweeping her up into his arms and lifting her in a circle. The golden dress fans out around her legs and reflects the firelight in every stone sewn onto it. "That was amazing!"

"No thanks to you." The moment her feet are back on the ground, I shoulder my way between them. My palm meets with Cassius' chest. He encouraged this and she almost got hurt because of it. I shouldn't have ever let her take the dare.

"She's fine, Black." He laughs and brushes my hand away from his chest as though I'm little more than a speck of dust.

"And she almost *wasn't*. You encouraged her to do this and then when she nearly slipped and fell, where were you? I sure as hell didn't see you falling over yourself to help." My voice raises enough that the room quiets, attention drawing to me. Every part of my body burns. My face must be crimson with the way magic pulses inside of me, heating every cell.

"It's only a game. *She* accepted the dare."

"She might be dumb enough to take the dare but we know better than to let it get that far. You know better than to encourage it." My fist would feel so good colliding with Cassius' face right now. We've always run in the same circles and been friendly enough. Not to mention, Sonnet is supposed to be a means to an end. So why does my chest ache so terribly at the idea of giving her and her innocence away to such a man?

"Malcom, I'm fine," Sonnet hisses at my side.

"Don't be stupid, Poesy, you could have gotten seriously injured." I can't even turn to look at her.

"Do not," her voice wobbles, "call me stupid." The hurt in her tone is evident and I can't avoid looking at her then. Wild strands of hair, pulled free from the wind, curl around her face. Those full lips are parted on a breath, cherry kissed from the cold. Her sea-stained eyes are glassy, echoing her hurt. The same feeling begins to throb inside my chest. "Now, if you all would excuse me," her eyes never leave mine, "I think I'll take my leave."

"Oh, Sonnet," Trudy coos at her side before sweeping her into a hug. Sonnet hands her the green gem as proof of the completed dare before gathering her skirts and hurrying from the room.

The door clicks shut and it's silent for only a second before the group starts chatting again as if nothing even happened. Someone shouts that they'll take truth but I don't even hear the question as my pulse pounds inside my ears. Cassius

grips my shoulder, mumbling some artificial plat-
itudes before turning away from me.

What did I just do? Fuck.

Not a soul notices as I hurry toward the
door. Once again, I've gone and messed everything up. I let my mouth and my anger get the
better of me. I didn't really mean it. Sonnet isn't
dumb. She only wanted to fit in and have some
fun. I've done worse things on a dare. It's all
part of the fun. Maybe it's this blood oath that
makes me feel so possessive of her. My need to
keep her safe so she can fulfill her part of the
bargain. That must be why I've suddenly lost all
sense.

The Hollis' halls are a blur in my periphery as
I race through the home following the short clip
of heels against the wood. "Poesy!" I call as I
round a corner and see the dress I'd bought her
glistening at the end of the hall. She doesn't stop
though. She hardly even gives me a glance over
her shoulder as she continues marching away.

"Poesy, please," I practically demand,
catching up enough to grab her shoulder and
pull her to a stop.

Sonnet bats my hand away as violently as
she'd kicked the plants away from her in the
Bitten Woods, but then her finger is jabbing into
my chest. Annoyingly familiar. "*You,*" she
seethes, "are supposed to be helping me." Her

eyes darken to an evening storm, hate pooling in their depths.

"I—"

Sonnet turns on her heels and starts off again. I snap my jaw closed, huffing a hot breath out through my nose. How are we supposed to work together when we can't even talk? She won't even let me talk. Pulled behind her, either by my guilt, anger, or possibly the blood oath itself, I stay at her heels until we're outside and I can practically see the heat rising off her skin. I'm sure I'm no better as my blood is nearly boiling within me.

"Can you just let me speak?" I snap with a stomp of my foot. The movement feels childish but it's too late to take it back.

The whites of her eyes are exposed as she rolls her gaze up to the clouds. "Don't you think you've said enough?"

"No. I mean, yes, but no." Pinching the bridge of my nose, I take a second to compose myself. Apologies are fucking hard, but I spoke out of turn, even if I think taking that dare was possibly the dumbest thing I've ever seen. "I'm —" Damn just spit it out, Malcom. "I'm sorry. I shouldn't have called you dumb or stupid." I straighten. "And you shouldn't have taken that dare."

I swear her eye twitches. "You know you almost had it. You were this close." She pinches her fingers together. "Nearly a half-decent apology and you go and ruin it with that." A shiver runs through her as she cups her arms around her body. She didn't grab her coat on the way out, and goosebumps trail across her flesh.

A muscle ticks in my jaw. Shrugging out of my suit jacket, I thrust it into her arms. "I know you want to prove yourself but you almost got seriously hurt. If I hadn't been paying attention, you'd be a puddle in the yard." I gesture to the grass at our side. "I saved you from yourself."

"I do not need to be saved."

"Sure, next time, I'll let you fall."

"Let us not forget that it is you who needs me." Sonnet's full lips are pulled downward but she slips her arms into my jacket and hugs the material around her.

I fold my arms over my chest. "This arrangement is mutually beneficial."

"I didn't need you to save me and I don't need you to complete my list."

"Sure, keep telling yourself that, Poesy."

"My name is Sonnet." Her arm raises, finger extended, surely ready to aggressively poke me again as she takes a step forward. I close the space and grab her hand in mine, curling my grip around her slender fingers.

"Sonnet. Poesy. Same difference."

Her breaths come rapidly, her chest rising to

brush against my abdomen. A strand of black hair blows across her cheek as she cranes her neck to look up at me. My eyes dance from her hardened gaze down to her mouth. Inside my chest, my heart beats violently, fueled by frustration and something else I'd rather ignore. My body moves on its own accord, closing the space between us until our breaths mingle and I can smell the lingering scent of wine on her tongue. Sonnet blinks up at me. Her lashes flutter before she deflates and slowly pulls her hand from mine.

"Thank you for saving me," she says quietly.

"I'm sorry. I didn't hear that; can you say it again?"

"Thank you." She takes a step back. "For saving me."

"My ears might be clogged because I still didn't catch it. One more time."

She swats my arm. Eyes round in warning. "Malcom."

A chuckle manages to escape me. "You're welcome. I really am sorry though for calling you stupid."

"No, it was stupid. I'm more upset that you said it in front of Cassius."

Right. Because she likes him. She wants to catch his eye. And I agreed to help her.

"A mistake I won't make again." Gravel

crunches under my boots as I lower into a bow. "I'll make it up to you." Her chin dips into a nod as a carriage pulls around the side of the building for her. "And I'll see you tomorrow?"

"Tomorrow."

Her carriage rolls to a stop behind her. She's the first to break eye contact as she turns and takes her footman's hand. Sonnet doesn't even turn to look at me as she's driven away still wearing my jacket. Somehow, though, I can't stop watching her. Even as the carriage turns down the street the ghost of our conversation lingers with me. The feeling of having her body so near mine and those dangerously devious eyes watching me holds me captive.

Sonnet Weatherwood might just be more than I bargained up for.

Sonnet

"I could have picked you up from your house," Malcom says, holding the carriage door open.

My father's old blacksmith shop sits empty behind us, the windows covered in a thick layer of dust, a for sale sign faded and crooked in the window. It's a quaint, blue building with violet trim. I distinctly remember my mother carefully painting the trim, not because she had to, but because she wanted to. Something to make a boring shop look a little bit livelier, she'd said. That was when I was still so young that I got scowled at every time I stepped foot behind the front counter for fear that I would make it to the back of the shop where Father did his work, and I'd get burned.

Had I been born a man I might have been

trained up to take over the blacksmith business. That would have helped us immensely after the accident that killed Mother and crippled Father for the rest of his life. I'd make much more money as a blacksmith than as the assistant to Daydale's physician. Yet, I was born into a different role created by our carefully balanced society, so really, it's society's fault that I'm in this position now in the backseat of a dazzling carriage preparing to commit a crime.

"Here is great." My navy dress fans out against the seat as I plop myself onto the cushion. It's work not to groan as my body sinks into the fine materials of the seat.

"Do you secretly live in a shack in the woods like a witch? Or is your home just three shingles tied together with twine?" The carriage door snicks shut.

I scoff. "No."

"I have your address. I sent you dresses, remember? I could go and look for myself."

Groaning, I let my head lull toward him. "I wish you wouldn't."

The carriage shudders into movement, rocking forward as Malcom sits himself across from me. He scratches at the slightest amount of stubble that's grown on his chin. His brown eyes look more like melted caramel, somehow brightened by his maroon coat and pants. Crossing an ankle over his knee, he leans back in his seat and spreads his arms across the back, watching me.

"Why?"

Sighing, I let my hands flop down at my sides. "What if my father has a skin condition that makes him look like a werewolf?"

Malcom barks a laugh. "Poesy, I've met your father. He has no such thing."

"Oh. Right."

"We met at the Hollis' party, and even before that, he made me a sword, perhaps two years ago. It's quite attractive and the blade has held up splendidly. He does good work. I'm sad that he doesn't take projects anymore." He locks eyes with me. "All to say he has no conditions that are so obvious."

"Fine, you caught me." I guess I can't pretend my father is a werewolf then. How inconvenient.

Flickering lamp lights outside go past through the slightly parted curtains over the windows. It all only exists in my periphery though as I sit locked within Malcom's attention.

"What's the real reason you don't want me to see your home?"

I clasp my hands in the ridiculously nice seat and refuse to look away from his heated gaze. "Let's talk about something else. Like how you could sell this ridiculously expensive carriage and pay off your debt just as easily. Is the detailing in here pure gold?"

His other eyebrow joins the first, rising until they are both hidden under the swoop of icy white hair. "They are. Interesting idea. Wouldn't work though. You don't think my father would notice we're down a carriage?"

I'm sure they have several carriages. Would his father *really* notice if one of them disappeared?

"You could try telling your father the truth." I purse my lips knowing it's a long shot.

"And end up disowned and living on the streets. No, thank you."

"Honesty is good for the soul."

He cocks his head watching me. "Maybe I don't have one."

"A soul?"

He nods slowly.

I give him a small smile. His eyes break their hold on mine to dip down to my lips. "You saved me. I think that means that you do in fact have a soul."

"Don't mistake that for kindness or care. I need you to help me. Nothing more." He folds his hands in his lap.

"If you say so." Somewhere deep in the terrible depths of the man someone decent resides even if he refuses to admit it. I only need to pry his goodness out of him.

"Did you memorize the plan?" he continues.

"Yes. And then I burned it." Which felt incredibly dramatic and unnecessary. Who would be looking through my crumbled rubbish? No one.

He rubs his palms together. "Perfect. Nervous?"

"Not at all," I say while feeling perspiration already running down the length of my dress. My heart has felt like a stuttering mess all day waiting for evening to come. I've replayed every way this could go wrong in my head over and over again. Working at Dr. Lowen's office I even drew a doodle of what I might look like behind bars. It's not pretty. I'm a terrible artist, and I'll never suit a prison cell.

"It'll all be fine, and I'll get you back home to your family...or to the shop before you know it."

I really can't believe I'm doing this.

After several quiet minutes, our ride comes to a stop, jostling our knees together. I pull myself back into my seat giving him as much space as possible, lest he infect me with whatever disease makes him think being a criminal is a good idea.

"Ready?" He leans forward, closing what

little space I'd given us. My heartbeat ticks faster, and my breath catches in my chest.

The carriage door is pulled open before I can answer. My saving grace. Voices trickle in. Silhouettes of bodies outlined by the theatre lights as people make their way inside the building. My heartbeat quickens in my chest.

"Allow me." He waves off the footman, stepping out of the carriage and lifting a hand to me.

I stare at his palm. The hands I remember being on my body, firm but not calloused. There is no going back now. The thrum of that bargain that's bonded to my very being reminds me. So, I force myself to inhale and slip my hand into his. Warmth unfurls in my core as our skin meets. His eyes darken, but otherwise, Malcom looks unaffected by the contact. It's only me that gets this flutter of nervous energy, apparently. And it's only because I'm about to venture into deplorable territory. Taking his hand is inviting scandal.

Behind us the theatre stands several stories high, curtains pulled closed on the other side of the wide windows set under archways molded and shaped to look like dragons breathing out fire. The stones of the building were once a light cream color but have since aged and darkened to almost black. The open red doors, parted to reveal the staircase that leads to the seats, look as though we're about to walk into the mouth of the dragon itself. I'm about to be swallowed whole and I can't do anything to stop it.

"Smile, Poesy, you look as though you've seen a ghost," Malcom says under his breath. My hand is still trapped in his and he gives me a reassuring squeeze before letting it go. "Let's go make our presence known."

Which takes all of three seconds to manage as I turn around to see Trudy Hollis rushing in my direction. Her arms wrap around me in a hug as she tugs me close against her. "Why didn't you tell me you were coming to the theatre? We could have ridden over together."

"Oh, it was a last-minute thing," I answer somewhere in the nest of her hair. The strands tickle my face and threaten to get sucked into my mouth as I inhale.

She pulls away, glancing at my plain, very last-season dress, and her smile tightens. "I can tell." Malcom clears his throat at my side and Trudy's attention drifts up and then up some more until she finally realizes who's standing with me. "Oh," she whispers, then clears her throat and beams. "It was so lovely seeing you. I hope you enjoy the show. I've heard people are absolutely raving over it." Trudy's eyes widen as she gives me a look of pure excitement before she touches my shoulder and squeezes a little before running off in the direction she'd come.

"Well, now that *she's* seen us everyone will know we're here. Makes this easier on us, I suppose." He offers his arm. "Come, let's head to my family's box. Cassius' family has a box next to ours; you never know, he might be lingering about like an incurable disease."

My stomach does a flip and a flop at the idea. Maybe I should have demanded that Malcom provide me with dresses for all these occasions. The idea of Cassius seeing me as I am now has me digging my teeth into my cheek. Still, I gently let my hand hover against Malcom's arm.

The tap of my heels muffles when I step into the theatre. Crimson carpets and curtains offset the old graying stones. Two stone dragons are perched at the end of the grand staircase that leads to the second level, both with their front two claw-tipped paws curving around the hilt of a short sword. As a child, I'd been scolded when I'd tried to climb onto the back of one of the dragons. Then I got to relive that experience when my sister was old enough to tag along and she tried to do the same. I touch the end of my fingers to the cold stone head.

Malcom waves and politely says hi to several people as we walk to our seats. Once upon a time, we'd come to the theatre monthly, but we'd always sat as a family on the first floor. I'd wondered on more than one occasion what the view from the boxes over our heads looked like and today I'll finally find out.

The staircase narrows and twists to the right. We move with the throngs of people all going to find their own seats. Lights dim the farther we climb, only a few golden sconces every few feet to guide our way. When the stairs come to an end, we find ourselves in a hallway lined with doors. Some are propped open, people moving in and out chatting amongst themselves before the show starts. Others are still closed, including the door we stop in front of.

"After you." Malcom twists the knob and pushes the door wide to reveal a set of six over-stuffed chairs lined before the balcony over-looking center stage.

My jaw drops open, and my gaze immediately goes to the curtains with the golden ropes draped across them where the show is about to take place. I'm looking out at the view and the people all finding their seats below us, so I don't notice the bar cart kept at the back of the box until Malcom hands me a short glass of clear liquid. At first, I assume it's water until I take a sip and I have to cover my mouth with a hand to keep from spitting it out.

"Liquor. To steady the nerves." He lifts his

own cup ever so slightly in salute before he down the contents.

"I'm not nervous." I sip the drink again with a crinkle of my nose and walk slowly toward the balcony railing. People need to see us; they need to see *me* in this box.

"Right." Malcom hums. "I'll be right back. There are a few more people I want to make my presence known to. Take a seat, enjoy the drink."

He's gone in a flash of movement, leaving the door to the box open behind him. Just me, my thoughts, and this terrible drink. I lean against the balcony railing. The ceiling itself is an art piece. I'd always given myself a neckache looking up at it from below. Dragons with gold scales and wings of white angel-like feathers blow orange flames across the blue sky backdrop. From the balcony, I can almost see each and every brushstroke and I wonder how long it took the artist to complete such a detailed piece. The entire image comes to a pinpoint at the center where a chandelier hangs, the color of the dragon's flames with hints of white and blue as though the fire itself is only moments from dripping down onto the unsuspecting crowd. I lean a little farther wondering if I might get close enough to reach out and touch the chandelier.

"Careful now, you wouldn't want to fall," a man's voice calls to me.

I startle and the liquid in my glass sloshes. With a glance about the box, I confirm I'm still alone, so I stretch out enough to see beyond the walls that separate this space from the next to find Cassius leaning against his own balcony railing to my left.

"I've seen someone dangle from the edge once, but they were pulled back up rather quickly. I'd hate to see something so dangerous happen to a pretty girl like you. Especially after your recent scare." His brilliant white teeth flash in a flirtatious smile. "What are you doing in the Black's box? Shouldn't you be over here with me?"

Yes, I wish.

"Last minute invitation from Malcom, but maybe for another showing you could invite me over. I'd love to see the view from your box." Wow, my flirting skills need some practice, I think, feeling the tips of my ears turn hot.

"Now that sounds like a plan. Or should I say a date? Unless you and Malcom have something going on?"

The man looks stunning in his baby blue dress shirt, rolled up to his elbows, and tucked into navy trousers. And he's even turning to charming coquetry with me.

Perhaps I am good at being a criminal

because I feel like I've spun a web and caught Cassius Calloway unsuspecting within it.

"Oh, no," I rush to say. "Malcom and I are more like siblings. He's a good friend, practically my brother." Then I give a nervous laugh that I wish I could take back as soon as it's left me.

Like a brother? I mean that's one way to let Cassius know I'm not interested in Malcom, but the hot tingling feeling I get when Malcom is near is *not* how one should feel toward their brother. At least I hope, I only have a sister and she's never given me the flutters. Food poisoning once, but nothing akin to butterflies in my stomach.

"I'll admit I am happy to hear that." He gives a deep chuckle. Even his laugh is attractive.

"And I'm happy to hear that you're happy."

"Why are we so very happy?" Malcom appears beside me, leaning out farther to dare a glimpse at who I'm speaking to. The balcony railing groans a little as he presses his weight into it.

"Sonnet says you too are good friends. *Just* good friends," Cassius says, part of his smile falling. "Practically siblings."

"Ah, yes, like a little sister, this one." And then he takes one hand and ruffles my hair. He ruffles it! Not that I'd done anything too special to it, but I know that tufts of frizz are standing on edge now. As sneakily as I can, I slide my elbow into his ribs. He grunts.

Thankfully, I'm saved from having to come up with something that could recover this situation because a strum of music comes from the orchestra below the stage and the heavy curtains flutter. Malcom gives Cassius a short wave and Cassius gives me a quiet nod before we step back and lower ourselves into our seats.

Malcom gives us a total of two minutes; enough time for me to watch the curtains open and a single dancer, dressed like a nutcracker, makes his way out and leaps then spins about the stage. He stands, tilts his head toward the door, and says, "Let's go."

Silently, we creep out of the theatre through a service entrance I hadn't even known existed, a notch in a wall that opens like a door to an even darker staircase. I curse my echoing steps as we make our way down the spiraling steps. Eventually, we're spit out on the backside of the theatre into a small alleyway where Malcom reaches for a bag, pulls out black fabric, and thrusts it into my arms.

"What is this?" I hold up the cloth only to find a pair of trousers. A shirt drops onto the ground.

"Clothes."

"And what am I supposed to do with them?"

With one hand he pulls his shirt over his head. Moonlight alone shows off the ripple of muscles he's had hiding under there this entire time. I nearly gasp but manage to keep it in if only to deny him the satisfaction. Yes, he's handsome. And the man knows it. Which is confirmed by the little smirk he gives me. I shouldn't want to lick chocolate off his flat stomach, but my goodness, I do. The things I could do with my tongue to this man...

"Put them on."

"Now?!"

"Do you not know how?" He reaches for the buttons on his trousers.

"This was not outlined in your plan." I grit my teeth and turn in the opposite direction. Is he about to take his pants off in front of me? He's supposed to help me achieve the holiday of my dreams not ruin me!

"Sometimes you need to improvise, but I thought it would be easier for you to move about if you weren't in all those layers. Plus, this way if someone does see us it's not in the same outfits we were just seen in here."

He does make a good point. Perhaps he is better at this than I give him credit for. And if he is, then does he really need me after all?

"Get changed, Poesy, before I start stripping you out of your dress myself." His voice is gruff and threatening enough to spur me into action.

"Don't look."

There is shuffling behind me as he laughs quietly. "No promises."

Every muscle in my body stiffens at his words and I chance a look over my shoulder only to see the expanse of his back as he fiddles with the waist of black pants. Sighing in relief, I tug my sleeves, and the dress falls from my shoulders revealing my shift. I hurry to pull on the trousers. They were certainly made for a small man, but they fit well enough. With one more look to ensure that he's minding his own business, I pull my shift off and slip into the black collared shirt. The buttons are undone to expose my collarbones and the curve of my breasts. I make sure to button it up the rest of the way and hide any small glimpse of my pale skin.

"Ready?" Malcom asks.

I spin around and glare. He blinks, attention drawn to where my hands have gone to balance on my hips. "How long have you been watching?"

"Long enough to see that small scar on your back."

A mark from when I'd fallen out of a tree and managed to land directly on a rock. A much younger Dr. Lowen had stitched me back up.

"Don't you ever listen?" I hiss.

"I'm not known for it." He smirks, bending to gather our clothes only to shove them back into the bag and hide it behind a waste bin. "Follow me."

The retort on my tongue will have to wait because he turns so abruptly to disappear around the corner, I have no choice but to follow. Then my nerves get the better of me because I don't do much more than shallowly breathe as we weave through side streets and shadows together. Several times, Malcom looks back at me or beckons me in one direction or the other.

Evening air moves through the thin clothing he'd given me. Never would I have thought I'd miss the layers of my dress, but the material is a lot thicker than this. Goosebumps chase up my arms with every gust of wind that howls through the rows of homes.

"There." He stops and points toward a large brick house. Lights are on in every window which causes my brows to pinch together as I look at him as though he's insane, which I'm pretty sure he is. That look only lasts so long as I take another perusal of the property I'm about to break into and notice the name carved into the stones of the gate that separate the property from the others.

Calloway.
You've got to be kidding me.

SONNET

"They won't notice it's missing anyway," Malcom says so softly I hardly catch his whispers.

I shake my head once but that isn't enough to stop him from gripping my wrist and dragging me with him along the iron fencing. Rocks skitter around us as I dig my heels in. His strength proves to be greater though as I'm merely tugged along like a child.

The Calloways?! A flood of anger is hot in my chest and pulsing inside of my skull. The one family I'm trying to get in the good graces of and Malcom really picked them to be his target? I shouldn't be surprised. Malcom is a terrible heartless creature, after all.

"You're going to steal from your friend?" I whisper-hiss back.

Tingles work their way up my spine. A warning. A pull on the blood oath that binds me to him. Most abhorrently, a reminder that no matter what, I'm breaking into this home today and leaving with whatever Malcom needs to cover his gambling debts.

"To be clear, we are not friends. More like begrudging acquaintances."

Large, incredibly old trees reach toward the sky, as tall as at least ten three-story homes stacked on top of each other. They loom over the brick home like ancient guardians. I get my feet under me and brush my palm against thick gnarled bark, thankful that these trees aren't the kind to take a bite out of you. Though every moment we linger under the branches, my skin crawls with the sensation of being watched.

The back of the house is much darker than the front. From this side, it looks as if the home is blessedly empty. Not a single light in any window nor a flicker of movement. I let out a slow breath. Maybe I can do this. Maybe.

"I paid a servant to leave the back door unlocked. The entire family is at the theatre and only the housekeeper and butler remain, but they should both be in their quarters at this time. Stay quiet and follow me." He beckons me forward with a wave of his hand.

"I hate you," I whisper in his direction earning myself a roll of his brown eyes.

"There's a fine line between hate and love, Poesy. Better be careful lest you fall in love with me."

My frown deepens to a scowl. "You don't have to worry about that."

In love? With him? Never. Lust, maybe. There is no denying the way my body reacts to him, but that has nothing to do with love.

Though the trees mask us from the light of the moon and our clothes help to hide us in the dark, I still feel exposed creeping through the Calloways' back gates. My eyes sweep over every corner, every sway of the shadows as the window blows the branches overhead. I fist my trembling hands at my sides as we take quiet steps up to the servants' entrance.

Malcom exhales as he twists the knob and pushes the door. It opens without a sound and he gives me a wink before taking a step inside. There's no outrunning this deal. So, no matter how bad I want to turn and sprint for the hills, I take a step inside.

A sliver of light comes from the other room, barely enough for me to make out the small hall that leads into the kitchen. From there, I know we'll find a staircase to the second floor which will lead us to bedrooms. One of which keeps something very valuable in it. This I only know from the messily drawn picture Malcom had made on the note he'd given me that's only artfully depicted within my mind's eye.

The Calloways' home smells faintly of vinegar but mostly like warm bread. My stomach growls and I pat my hand against it as if that might keep it silent. The rest of the house is quiet, lending to the thought that everyone is either gone or in their own quarters. It's enough to help me relax as we slip through the kitchen and up into the stairway.

Underfoot a stair creaks. I freeze. Eyes wide, Malcom turns and points to where he's climbing the steps with his feet only on the outer edges near the wall. I mimic the motion, wincing when the wood groans again. I *never* said I was good at breaking and entering. *Great, now I'm picturing myself in a cell again. I'm going to be sick.* My fingers smooth over the wallpaper as I follow closely behind. He pauses at the top of the stairs listening for seconds that feel more like years as my pulse races.

One dip of his chin, and he's pushing through yet another door. On this floor, a few sconces have been lit. Even this tiny bit of light is too much. Malcom doesn't seem to care though as he stalks forward. A gentle hum comes from another hall. My heart leaps into my throat, choking out any room for me to breathe.

"Fuck," Malcom says under his breath. "Inside. Now."

Taking my wrist, he practically tosses me into the bedroom. I only have enough time to make out the shape of a massive four-post bed, a small bookcase, a desk, and two armchairs in front of an empty fireplace before Malcom's hand presses between my shoulders and thrusts us into a closet. The door closes with a soft click. My back hits a wall and layers of hanging clothes dig into my arms, hangers momentarily jangling together. Malcom's weight aligns against me.

"What are you doing?" I half whisper, half sneer.

"Shh." His finger presses against my lips. I contemplate biting it. I want to, really, truly want to. But I don't. Not when I hear the door to the bedroom open and close and the person humming enter the room.

This is wrong. We're crazy, aren't we? We have to be. We should both be admitted to some sort of hospital. Preferably separate hospitals so I don't ever have to see his smug face again.

His finger lowers from my mouth, both his hands finding my hips and holding me snugly against him. Even his head is bowed over me as he hunches into the small space. Those long fingers curl against me, squeezing against the waist of the borrowed trousers. With every breath we take our chests rise and fall against each other. The strong musk of him is enough to keep me from feeling sick with the strong scent of mothballs. It's enough to make me want to get drunk on him. Why does he have to smell so good? The gods couldn't stop at him being beautiful and rich; they made sure that his scent was as delectable.

The shuffle of movement starts and stops. Humming coming and going then changing tunes. I stare up at him contemplating how I'll get him back if we're caught.

"Don't look at me like that, Poesy." His lips move against my temple.

"Like what?" I can hardly even hear myself I speak so quietly.

"Like you can't decide if you want to kiss me or kill me." His lips turn up, the movement soft, yet noticeable, against my skin. "You act like I'm a monster but perhaps part of you likes that."

I huff. He has no idea what he's talking about. I press my lips together and his attention dips down to the movement. Outside the closet, the humming continues but moves farther away. Distantly, a door opens and closes muting the sound further.

Together, we stand in the closet, bodies

pressed close, breaths mingling, and eyes locked. We stay like that for several long minutes giving my body time to warm and for something dangerously pleasant to bloom deep within me.

"Okay, I think it's safe." Malcom pulls away, taking within him that budding sensation.

When we step out of the closet, the room is lit with a fire now roaring in the fireplace. I take a second to take in my surroundings. Now, I can clearly see the large blue quilt thrown across the massive bed. A book sits open but facedown on a small nightstand next to it. To my right, the desk is neatly organized, a parchment pulled out with quill and ink at the ready. My fingers dance over the items, a letter unopened and addressed to Cassius has me snatching my hand back.

This is Cassius' room?!

Turning, I give Malcom my best glare. Not that he cares, because he's running his hands around the edge of a landscape painting as tall as him, mumbling to himself. "Here it is." There's a click and then the picture swings forward on hinges like a door to reveal a hole a fraction of the width of a regular door.

"There she is!" Malcom waves an arm toward the hole before settling his hands proudly on his hips. "Cassius is such a proud bastard. Get him drunk and the man will boast about anything including where he hides all the money his father

doesn't know about. And in there is my debt."
He points a finger at me. "This is where you
come in."

"Me?" I ask as if I'm unaware that I'm actually supposed to play a part here. I've tried rather
hard not to think about it. This is the part where
Malcom's plan became rather vague. More like a
'get the money and get out' sort of thing rather
than a 'Sonnet is supposed to go inside a tiny
door' thing.

"You think my muscular frame is going to
fit?" He emphasizes his point by flexing.

Gross. "I'd run through fire to never have to
watch you do *that* again."

"In you go." He pushes the painting further
open.

Everything past the impossibly small gaping
hole is black. I pause at the entrance trying and
failing to see anything. "And what exactly am I
going into?"

"Oh. Right." With the snap of his fingers, a
small flame appears in his palm. So, he has some
sort of fire magic. Interesting. That explains why
he didn't need so many layers when he was lying
in the snow when we met. It also explains why I
always feel so warm when he is close.

He holds his hand out letting it light the
space beyond ever so slightly. Shelves line either
side of the wall going several feet back. Stacks of

money, jewels, small chests, and some books even are neatly organized. "You're looking for a ring. Slim gold band. A large diamond with two small diamonds on either side."

My eyes narrow. "A ring? I thought you needed money."

"Yes, well said ring is valuable." He looks at the floor. "It's also a family heirloom."

"You gambled a family heirloom?"

"I—"

"Actually"—I hold up a hand—"don't say anything. The less I know the better. Let's get this done." The doorway and tiny alcove beyond are hardly anything special. Just another small closet hidden behind a picture. Yet it holds more wealth than my family has seen in months.

I suck in, trying to make myself as small as possible, and my breasts still feel as though they are being crushed against my body as I slide through the cramped doorway. Malcom leans in after me, offering the light in his palm.

"Closer please." His hand juts in farther. I lift myself on my toes, eyes trailing over coins, paper money, and trinkets. I blow out and dust lifts from the top shelf. It's organized in here, but he clearly doesn't come in much. Pulling my hands back so I don't leave fingerprints, I continue my perusal.

To have this much wealth while those

without magic struggle to make ends meet makes my stomach twist and turn until it feels like it's in a knot. Once, I'd lived a life so similar, not quite this excessive, but close. It's the life I'm fighting to get back now. Silently, I vow that if we ever have the money again, I'll help those like me. Fae born without abilities. Fae who are punished for existing in bodies they didn't ask to be born into.

"The ring, Sonnet. We don't have all night."

"I'd like to see you squeeze in here and try to find a ring you've never seen before without knocking everything off the shelves like a bumbling idiot," I snap back.

After another shelf with no gold banded ring on it, I bend to try and look lower, careful not to back myself up into another shelf. Malcom lowers his flame to follow my movement. Light glints off something drawing my attention. Carefully, I stretch my arm to the back only running my fingers over the fine piece of jewelry and picking it up. One obscenely large diamond somehow balances on a slender gold band, two practically as obnoxiously sized diamonds framing it on either side. I palm the ring. When he said it was valuable he wasn't kidding. This must cost more than everything in my home is even worth.

A glowing warmth radiates off the ring. I glance back at Malcom to see if he's brought the fire closer yet, but he hasn't moved. The ring lets off its own light, shining impossibly bright inside the closet. Part of me is terrified that it's some sort of magic placed on this room in case something is stolen so I close my fingers around it. Beams of light shoot through the space between my fingers, streaking across the shelves. I turn toward the door, holding my breath tightly as I push myself through the frame. All the while the ring grows hotter until it's a painful blistering heat within my palm.

"Ah!" I gasp letting it fall from my hand and onto the floor before Malcom. A perfect circle mars my flesh, red and angry. "It burned me."

"It...burned you?" I didn't think Malcom's coloring could turn any paler, but I was wrong. Every ounce of blood seems to drain from his face. Slowly, he bends down to pick it up. He doesn't so much as wince or seem bothered by the odd heat that had hurt me moments before. The light that had shone from it is gone. He inspects the ring for a moment and then pockets it.

"Do you think Cassius charmed it?"

"Hmm?" His brows pinch. "Oh. Maybe." He turns away, carefully lowering the picture back into place. He does all of it without so much as looking in my direction. I stole him back his family heirloom, burning myself in the process, and he can't even look me in the eyes?

"Can we leave now?" I fold my arms across my chest. My side of this bargain is over. He has much more left to fulfill.

Malcom dips his chin in a quick nod, his steps closing the space between us and the exit. I follow along feeling somehow lost to what actually happened. I just want to get this over with though, so I stay at his back, quiet, all the way back through the Calloways' home and through the dark evening streets of Daydale until I'm back in my theatre clothes and we're emerging from the service stairway at the back of the Black's box.

A woman belts a song as the male dancer from the beginning of the performance prances around her. A shadow shifts before the couple. I blink making out the silhouette of a man already seated in the box. Every hair on my body stands at attention. Malcom slows behind me, closing the hidden door.

The shadow stands, light coming into the box revealing curling blond hair. "Where have you two been?" Cassius Calloway asks.

MALCOM

Cassius fucking Calloway.

If I could count on my hands how many times this man has made my life harder, then I'd have way more than ten fingers. Now here he is, strolling from the shadows of my family's *private* box and looking at Sonnet with a possessiveness that makes anger flare to life within my shriveled black heart.

Cassius fucking Calloway.

My hand skims against the material of my pocket where my family's ring sits safely tucked away and I watch as the back of Sonnet's neck turns a delicate shade of red. Her body tenses as she slows to a stop before me. I let the servants' door close with a definitive click before flashing a smile at Cassius as though I'm not thinking about tossing him over the balcony right now. Though the urge is strong, and it would be immensely satisfying to see him tumble down to the first level, I restrain myself. Sonnet should be proud.

"She was curious about the servants' entrances. So, we gave ourselves a little tour. Could be useful knowledge if I ever wanted to sneak around one day." I slide past her, my chest brushing against her arm, then make my way to one of the seats and lower myself onto it. Her sweet scent fills the booth and it's an effort for me not to stop and greedily breathe her in.

Cassius' gaze shifts from me to Sonnet and he makes a show of dusting some lint off his jacket sleeve before straightening his cuff. "Hmmm, I worry your absence could give people the wrong impression. Not to worry though, I won't tell a soul."

All to say that no secret is ever safe with him.

"Impressions are merely assumptions, and what you so kindly have pointed out would be an incorrect assumption. Malcom and I are and will never be more than friends," Sonnet says, her tone serious but soothing.

The quickness with which Sonnet responds does something unsettling to my stomach. Nausea and annoyance mingle and rise like acid in the back of my throat. *Deny us, sure, but don't make it sound as though you've never stared at me as though you're contemplating what it might be like to be bedded by me.*

"It's important to keep in mind how society perceives you. Though I trust that you might only have eyes for one man." He takes a long step forward. His wide frame blocks out my view of Sonnet, not that I want to be watching them make eyes at each other anyway. Insufferable.

I force myself to look down at the stage in time to watch the male dancer take the queen into his embrace and plant a kiss right on her lips. The curtains close. Red fabric falling to cover the actors in one quick swoop of color only to be drawn open again as the crowd rises to their feet and the actors emerge to bow. I don't stand, but I do clap, even if slowly. Even over the roar of the crowd, I'm attuned to the voices behind me.

"Could I give you a ride home tonight, Miss Weatherwood?" Cassius practically purrs.

A sickness sits at the back of my throat waiting to be purged at the next flirty remark either of them makes. Sonnet wouldn't even let me pick her up from her house. I can't imagine she'd let Cassius take her home. Which is why my stomach flips when she says yes.

"That would be lovely," she answers. It takes everything in me not to turn around and glare at her. And if I were to get a glimpse of that pretty little smile pointed up at Cassius, I might actually set this damn chair on fire. Father would so hate to hear that I scorched the nice fabric in here.

The soft click of heels approaches from behind me. A gentle hand brushes against my forearm. Sonnet stands at my side, but I don't have it in me to even look at her. Instead, I keep my attention focused on the stage, clapping lazily as everyone gives their final bows and the crowd starts to turn from their seats.

"Thank you for bringing me to the show," she says quietly. All an act for Cassius.

If I didn't plan on forgetting all about her as soon as this bargain is done, I would consider bringing her back to watch a show. Something inside of me whispers in glee knowing she'd likely love it. Even if I am bored by the theatre, it might be worth watching her face as she takes it all in.

The most I can give her is a shallow nod. It's enough for her to turn away, back to Cassius' side where she takes his offered arm, and the pair strolls out together.

I close my eyes. Sighing, I press my palms to the back of my eyelids. The ring is heavy in my pocket. I should be happy, right? I've gotten my heirloom back. Father will never know, and no one else is the wiser. So why does my chest feel so damn achy?

And the ring...it'd burned hot and glowed when Sonnet had touched it. She'd thought it was some sort of anti-theft spell on Cassius' part. No, he's way too full of himself to think anyone could make it far enough to rob him, but I've heard of the ring doing such a thing. Until that moment, I've always thought it was a myth, a funny little thing my family said to make their stories more dramatic.

Because the ring only glows like that when it's in the hands of its future wearer.

Sonnet Weatherwood is rightfully mine.

Sonnet

The tension that had made the Black's box so stifling resolves the minute Cassius and I walk arm in arm out of the theatre. More than one person stops to have a brief but friendly chat with Cassius. I note how much more polite he is than Malcom who merely nods or waves and continues on his way. I also note how incredibly exhausting it is to have to paste a smile on my face and make small talk with so many people. Perhaps Malcom is onto something.

After the intense adrenaline that had been

coursing through my body and then spiking at the sight of Cassius, exhaustion is weighing on my shoulders, but I haven't gotten this far to give up now. I'm in with Cassius; I can tell by the way he looks at me. I might even have a chance at becoming his bride if I play my cards right. Everything I've ever wanted and everything my family needs could be solved by this one man. I try to summon some spark of happiness. Shouldn't that be what I'm feeling right now? In lieu of that though, there seems to only be this dark pit of...dread. What is wrong with me?

It all could very well be the guilt that sits like a dark kernel of regret in my chest. I'm quite literally walking with the man whose home I just robbed and am going to climb into his carriage. On second thought, perhaps I should have turned down the ride.

He can't know what we've done, I remind myself.

The carriage that pulls up in front of the theatre is a lot plainer than I expect. It's not the gaudy gold-trimmed thing that Malcom had picked me up in. Instead, it's a very simple white carriage with black detailing. Modest, even. I suppose he doesn't need a carriage to tell people that he's filthy rich; everyone already knows.

"After you." Cassius pulls open the door, giving me his hand to help me step up and through the door. The interior is simple with black velvet cushions and pristine white walls.

His tall lean body takes up significant room when he finally settles into the seat across from me. Or it could be that he sits with his limbs taking up as much room as he can manage to steal. His knees are set apart, trapping the sliver of space for my legs between his. As the carriage rolls forward, he bumps against me, grinning.

"I'm quite pleased you allowed me to bring you home. Well, almost home." He winks poking fun at my whispered request on the way out to be brought to my father's old shop where my carriage will be waiting for me.

"I am quite pleased you asked," I say with an almost genuine smile.

I've seen the inside of his bedroom, and he doesn't even know it.

I know where he sleeps.

I know what the book set open on his night-stand is titled.

I...I am creepy. This is creepy.

"You know, my desk has been rather full of invitations for all the upcoming Yuletide events. Will I be seeing you at any of them?"

Unlikely, seeing as my family's mail remains painfully empty of said invitations. I won't say that though. This is Cassius I'm speaking to. So instead, I answer, "I am quite busy preparing for this holiday season, so we will see what I'll be able to squeeze into my schedule."

I am busy, I try to reason with myself. I've got work to worry about and taking care of the house and my family. That's a lot. Still, I'd rather be gliding across a dance floor in Cassius' arms instead.

He leans forward, scooping up my hand that rests against my knee, and rubs his thumb over my knuckles. "I do hope you will be in attendance. This is the most wonderful time of the year after all."

"The most wonderful time of the year," I repeat, watching his touch linger against mine.

Cassius brings my hand up to his mouth, pressing his lips where his thumb had touched. "There is something special about you, Sonnet Weatherwood."

No there isn't, that terrible wayward part of my brain shouts. *I have no magic and I'm nothing special.*

Another part of me wants to chuckle. Because I have to wonder how many women he's said this to. Then lastly, there is the part of me that wishes that this were true and that he meant it.

In my conflicted silence he continues, "There is something about you that draws me in." He takes a strand of my bangs and twirls it around his finger. "It could be this raven hair or yours." His hand drops my hair and shifts for him to run his pointer finger against my lower lip. The soft pad of his finger sends a shiver down my spine. My mouth waters for his touch. Crystal blue eyes dip down to my chest. "Your body," he finishes in a whisper.

In the last few months, I've lost a significant amount of weight between grieving my mother and having much less money available to put food on the table. My curves have diminished, my breasts feeling more like two swollen bug bites than anything else. Still, I shudder at the suggestion of his words.

"You truly are so beautiful." His fingers interlace with mine. "I'm happy that I will not be in competition with Malcom to win your favor. Not that I feel as though he stands much of a chance."

"You flatter me." I stare at our locked hands. "Not that Malcom and I could *ever* be a thing, but why do you say he doesn't stand much of a chance?"

"He tends to keep to himself when he has the opportunity. I've seen him flirt with women and there are many who want what his family could give them, but so rarely does he do more than take them to bed. I know that *you* aren't like that. You're not a woman to be used and cast aside. You're the girl that needs to be courted."

"Malcom has never courted a woman?"

"Not in the sense that he intends to marry them." He traces a finger along my arm. The light touch makes me want to close my eyes and revel in the sensation.

"And"—I force myself to meet his gaze—"have you courted anyone with the intention of marrying them?"

Blond curls bounce as he shakes his head. "I've not met the right woman yet, but I am hopeful."

My heart skips a beat. Am I having a heart attack? Should I call Dr. Lowen when I get home?

"I've been meaning to ask." Somehow he's brought himself forward, one of his knees pressing in closer until I can feel the tug of my dress from the pressure. "Could I call on you sometime?"

I grin so wide that my cheeks start to hurt. "I think that sounds wonderful."

Guilt rises like a tidal wave inside of me. He doesn't know that I've stolen from him. This entire venture feels so much more manipulative than authentic. My mouth goes dry but when his grin widens, I tell myself that all of this will one day be worth it.

SONNET

Two weeks. Two weeks I've fretted. I've lost sleep getting up early to try and make sure my home is clean and taken care of as possible. For two whole weeks, I've waited eagerly for Cassius to call. Did I mention it's been two weeks?? Two weeks where I think I've slowly begun to lose my mind worrying about when he might finally show up to call on me. I've hardly eaten as the anticipation built up inside of me. All for nothing.

Not once did I hear from him or receive anything from him or so much as see him in passing. He's forgotten about me. He's gone into hiding. Or he's downright avoiding me. I've gone from worthy of being courted to forgettable in a matter of days. I know I'm nothing special, despite what he'd said, but it was nice for a moment to think that someone actually thought that about me.

Now the Yuletide Ball is approaching and invitations should be arriving soon. Perhaps I need to remind Cassius of my existence. It's with that thought that I pull myself out of my room and call for Edmund. Within minutes I'm in our carriage and strolling through the parts of Daydale I haven't seen in six months. Here, all the houses are larger and their gates taller. Yards are dotted with purposeful, abundant, landscaping and occasionally a fountain can be found at their center. Yuletide decorations are grand, fighting with every other house to stand out. Trees are wound up with glittering ropes and baubles. Wreaths and garlands claim every surface. Poinsettias brighten every doorstep.

I know that if I look around the next bend, I'll be able to see the home we'd once occupied. The home I'd grown up in only to be forced out the moment our family became magicless. I refuse to even glance at it. In part because of the bitterness that's chained itself around my heart and also because I can't bring myself to see how the new family that lives there has made changes to the place that had once been ours.

So, instead of watching beautiful home after beautiful home go by, I stare down at my hands. The circle where Malcom's family ring had burned my palm has healed, but in its wake, there is a slender silver scar. It's so light it reminds me of their family's very distinctive hair. I suppose my venture into criminal affairs has permanently changed me. I'll never be able to forget it even if I want to.

Only when my scar tingles and we come to a stop in front of the Black's home do I finally look up. My heart lurches into my throat. From the window, I can't even see how tall the home is. Four stories? Five? Edmund opens my door, revealing the rest of the Black's home. Six. It's a six-story home.

Dark brown brick rises high enough to completely block out the morning sun behind it. Green vines run up columns of the arching doorway. Cobbled stone leads me from the carriage to the large looming doors. Edmund lifts the brass door knocker and taps it loud enough that we hear it echo in the home beyond. His eyes shift to me, his thin lips lifting into an easy smile.

"Yes, can I help you?" A short mousy-looking man answers the door. The black uniform he wears is neatly pressed, his shoulders perfectly straight, and somehow even though we're practically the same height, it's as though he's looking down his nose at me.

"Hi." I clear my throat. I've never actually

called on a man before. "Hello, uh, I'm looking to speak to Mr. Black."

The mousy man blinks. "Senior? Or one of his sons?"

"Oh." A nervous chuckle bubbles out of me. "Malcom Black, that is."

"Right this way. Would you care for some tea or scones while you wait?" he asks, holding the door wide for me to enter. Edmund follows closely behind but as we reach the sitting room he waits outside the doorway.

"No thank you," I manage to say as I stroll forward, staring at the pristine white furniture. I always figured they would lean into using more black in their home given their last name but as it turns out they rather prefer the crisp white of their hair.

With that, the man turns on his heel and promptly walks from the room, leaving me alone to wonder if I'm allowed to actually sit on the furniture. How do they keep it all so white? Surely if I sit on it, I'll manage to darken it somehow.

Three long wooden upholstered couches all face each other. Centered is a circular wooden table with a lovely arrangement of flowers, their bright color standing out amongst the neutrals. I brush a finger over a red rose, the velvet petals perfectly opened.

"I think the flowers make the room look much less sterile, don't you?" Malcom leans against the doorway, wearing a billowing white cotton collared shirt, half tucked into the same brown trousers I'd seen him in when we'd made the blood oath. His white hair sticks out at odd angles as though he'd been running his fingers through it or had only just now managed to get himself out of bed. Overall, the look suits him. Messy, unkempt, and still somehow one of the most attractive men I've ever had the privilege of laying my eyes on.

"It's a nice touch." I straighten. "Are these couches meant to be sat on?"

"No, not really. We have another sitting room on the other side of the house we use more often. This is where Thomas brings guests that he doesn't believe we would want to stay long." I frown but he continues. "Why are you calling on me, Poesy?"

"Take me on a walk through the park," I say.

Malcom's brows rise to hide under the mess of his hair. "Is that a question or have you added this to your list of holiday demands?"

"It's a request, I suppose." I pull my slipping shawl a little closer to my body and clasp my hands in front of me.

"I would think you'd know this, seeing as you had to go outside in some capacity to even get here, but it's cold, and I don't want to shiver my ass off without good reason."

Ugh. Of course he wouldn't want to come. Too bad for him though; he doesn't have much of a choice anymore. Still, I melt a little, slouching with a dramatic exhale. "Please, Malcom." I try and bat my eyelashes at him, but he only rolls his eyes. "It's been like two weeks since Cassius said he would call on me and I haven't heard a thing from him. Invitations for his ball are going out soon and I need to make sure that he remembers who I am."

"He remembers you. You don't need to subject yourself to the cold." Malcom pulls himself away from the door, hands easily going into his pockets as he saunters in my direction. "I wouldn't let him forget about you. We have a deal, remember?" He holds up the hand where our blood oath was made.

"Right." I nod. "But to be sure, we should go have a little promenade around the park."

He groans, dragging a hand down his features. "Poesy, you could very well be the death of me."

"Well, don't die yet, I still need you." I point out and he gives me half of a smile.

"Give me five minutes and we can go. My carriage or yours?"

"We can take mine. Edmund is happy to join us. Right, Edmund?"

"Yes, Miss Weatherwood," Edmund calls back from outside the room.

"Well, I guess that settles that," Malcom mumbles. "I'll meet you in the carriage. Hurry along before Eames finds you in here and you get trapped in a conversation you don't want to be a part of."

Not needing to be told twice, I hurry back to my carriage, sliding back into my seat in triumph. Our carriage is nice, a little weathered after not being able to do much upkeep in the last several months, but it's hardly plain. Plus, pulling up in one of Malcom's gaudy-looking rides would garner a bunch of attention. I don't want to be known for being seen with Malcom. I only want people to know that Cassius is mine.

When the door opens and closes again a much bulkier-looking Malcom settles into the seat next to me. He's layered on several coats, a scarf, and even pulled a hat snuggly around his ears.

"Are you trying to disguise yourself? You look like some sort of puffer penguin." I'd only seen the fluffy little creatures once on a trip north where they'd been enclosed in a zoo of sorts, but Malcom does quite resemble them currently. How can he even move with all those layers?

"It's cold."

I squint at him. At this proximity I can see the clammy sheen of sweat on his face and the pink that kisses his nose but somehow not his cheeks. "Are you...ill?"

"No." He shakes his head and leans back into the seat, closing his eyes.

"The cold didn't bother you before. You know when you tried to rob me, and you were in hardly any clothing."

He cracks one eye. "If we can forget that ever happened that would be great...but I expended a lot of magic to stay warm. Too much fabric would have hindered me then. Not that less fabric helped in the long run. But the cold does bother me and excess use of magic to keep my body warm wears me down. So, bundling up it is. I need my energy for other things." He gives a suggestive wink and I scowl.

"Oh, I didn't know that." Not that it really changes anything. I stole for this man. He can handle being cold for a few hours.

"When I was younger, my mother used to bundle me up worse than this. My arms would jut out so that I couldn't lower them and I waddled more than walked. Eames used to roll me down hills in the snow laughing until he was wheezing. Mother was worried that too much cold would extinguish my abilities. Not that

that's how magic works at all but she's of an older generation."

My mouth tips up at the edges imagining a young Malcom drowning in winter clothing and tumbling down a snowy hill.

"Whenever it snowed on Yule, my mother would always take my sister and me sledding. Our old home had a nice slope in the backyard. Father would sit up on the back patio with a cup of coffee, watching us through the steam. It always dissolved into a snowball fight. I'd keep going until my fingers were red and numb and Father would make me stop."

"That sounds nice. We don't really celebrate Yule at my house."

My head snaps to the side so violently, I'm surprised it doesn't turn in a full circle. "You don't celebrate Yule?! It's the best holiday there is. What do you mean you *don't* celebrate?"

He breathes out a laugh. "We don't really do anything. It's just another day." He shrugs, and the movement must be hard in his double coats. "My family kind of does their own thing. We don't make a big deal out of it."

"Just another day," I sputter. "Just another day?! Malcom. This is Yule! It's winter solstice! It's a time to spend with your loved ones and gorge yourself on sweets."

"Yeah, I thought that for a little while. You

know when you're young and in school everyone talks about how excited they are. Even though my family had never done anything before I held out hope that they would. I even gave my family a list of toys I wanted. Top of that list was a little wooden figurine of a Court of Frost soldier." He pinches his fingers to show me the approximate five inches of height. "One of my friends had one and I was so jealous of them. Father never really believed toys were necessary, so we had very few. He'd rather us focus on swordplay, magic, and our studies of course. And when Yule came around...it was the same nothing. That hope only lasted a couple of years before I grew up and realized it wasn't going to happen. Yule is just another damn day. One I'm not particularly fond of anymore."

"Oh, that's so sad. My parents always showered us with gifts." Though this year will be painfully different, I'm determined to still make it work.

"Well, maybe your family loves you more than my family loves me." He says it with an air of apathy and slight amusement, but I can't help but feel sorry for him.

I lean my head on his shoulder. "You can come to my family's Yule."

And we sit like that in stillness and quiet, with my head on his overly cushioned shoulder, until we make it to the park a few minutes later. Malcom's exit from the carriage is a labor that has me laughing so hard I stumble out of the carriage myself, nearly falling before he hooks an arm around my waist and straightens me. Clouds drift over the dark blue sky, muting the sun just as the wind picks up. I fix my shawl on my shoulders and pull my shoulders back, giving him an appreciative grin.

"Shall we...promenade?" He motions to the path that winds through the park.

Keeping my hands very much to myself, lest people consider us an item, I start along the path. Several others are out this morning, some on horseback, others walking simply as we are. Couples stop to chat with one another under the large evergreen trees. Somewhere in the distance is the joyful hum of enthusiastic chatter.

Now that I'm not shielded from the wind, every bitter breeze cuts through my all-too-thin dress. I try and fail to suppress a shiver. Over my dead body will I let Malcom know that he was right and it's a bit too cold to be out here.

"It's so lovely out," I lie through my chattering teeth.

"Sure, if your idea of lovely is frostbite."

"It's practically a winter wonderland, Malcom."

He tugs his scarf up higher on his face until I

can only make out his brown eyes that darken to nearly black as he glares down at me. "Sure—"

"Oh goodness! There he is!" I squeak catching my first glimpse of Cassius on the other side of the park. Picking up my pace, I grab Malcom's arm and drag him along. I knew he'd be out here. The Calloways don't miss an opportunity to appear in public.

I slow only when we're within hearing range and then turn to Malcom. "Make me laugh."

"Make you—"

A barking, ridiculously, terribly forced laugh barges out of my throat. I laugh loudly, bending at the waist as though I'm about to slap my knee. When I look up at Malcom he's cringing. Okay, maybe I've overdone it, but then I look up and Cassius is heading in our direction with a petite blonde at his side. For half a second, I'm annoyed only to realize that the resemblance is too canny and the beautiful woman to his left is his sister. I let out a slow exhale.

"You sound like a hyena. Never make that sound again," Malcom whispers.

"Shut up." I jab him with my elbow, turning toward the Calloways.

Unlike Malcom, Cassius is one long, lean line of stunning winter fashion. A baby blue jacket is buttoned all the way up with a navy scarf wrapped into an intricate knot at the front of his neck. I wonder if Malcom feels ridiculous yet.

"Sonnet!" Cassius flashes one of his brilliant smiles, jogging a few steps to close the space between us. "And..." He leans forward squinting at the eyes glaring back at him. Malcom pulls his scarf down just a bit and Cassius inhales sharply. "Oh, Malcom. How are you both?"

"Better now that Edith is here." Malcom uses that confident, charming voice of his that he never uses with me and Edith gives a little giggle. *How precious.*

I look at her a little closer. The same curls as Cassius though hers are longer and pulled to one side. She has earmuffs on that match the tan fur of her coat. Her lips are full and cherry red like her wind-kissed cheeks. She's beautiful.

"Weather is quite nice today, isn't it?" she asks, those large doe eyes of hers never leaving Malcom's face.

"Sure, if your idea of nice is frostbite." I laugh repeating what Malcom had said to me not long ago. The others give a slight chuckle and Malcom only watches me with a sidelong glance.

Cassius pats his sister's shoulder. "This one loves the cold. I'd rather be cozied up by the fire. Nevertheless, she needs a chaperone, so here I am." He holds his gloved hands out helplessly.

"I love the cold," Malcom repeats.

My eyes nearly pop right out of my head as I turn to look at him. "I'd have never known that with how much clothing you have on right now."

"I brought extra layers in case you get cold. Here." Those eyes flare in annoyance as he strips off the top coat and roughly places it like a cape around my shoulders.

I'm two seconds from shrugging out of it and letting it land in the snow when Cassius jumps in to save this absolutely embarrassing conversation. "You look stunning today, Miss Weatherwood."

My face warms. "Thank you, Cassius. That's quite a compliment coming from you. And that's quite an outfit you've put together."

"I was hoping I might look good for you should we run into each other. I'm so sorry that I haven't been able to visit as I'd hoped. Mother has been so stressed with preparations for the Yuletide Ball that she's even roped me into prepping for it."

"That's quite alright. I understand. If your family ever needs any help, I'd be happy to be of service."

Malcom snorts a little. I refuse to look at him though.

"Oh, look! Paisley is here. Let's go say hi, Brother." Edith hooks her arm through Cassius' and pulls him away. He gives half a wave as he goes that I return a bit too eagerly.

The second I know they're out of earshot I shimmy out of Malcom's coat, letting it drop to the ground behind me. My eye twitches in annoyance as he huffs and picks it back up, shaking it out. "He is losing interest." And I can't help but dramatically emphasize my point with a snap of my fingers as my worry begins to seep out of me. I hope Cassius doesn't look back to see me having a minor freak-out. "You need to help secure my ticket." I lower my voice. "*I helped you steal from that man.*"

Picking off a small twig from his jacket, he looks up from under his brows at me. "You need to get in good with Edith too."

"Of course you would say that."

"Of course I would say what?"

"That you want me to spend time with Edith because *you* want to spend time with Edith."

"I don't want to spend time with Edith."

"Ah. Sorry. I must have been confused by your lovey-dovey heart eyes you were making at her," I snap.

"She's cute." He deadpans.

"So are kittens."

The two of us stand in the middle of the walkway frozen as we stare at each other. I want to slap one of his two hats right off his head.

He breaks the silence first and, honestly, it feels like another win on my part. "I do happen to know that she will be dress shopping tomorrow. You should also go dress shopping."

"Sure, Malcom, I'll just drop my life's savings to make sure to exist in the same place as Edith Calloway."

His sigh is almost as dramatic as my hand gestures. "Poesy, I'll pick you up tomorrow and you don't have to worry about the cost. Can we please go home now?"

He's going to buy me another dress? I did risk my entire reputation to help him get back that incredibly expensive-looking ring. I suppose that's fair enough.

SONNET

The little bell over Madame Collette's shop chimes overhead as Malcom ushers me inside. Baby pink wallpaper embossed with shiny pink roses covers the walls. Three floor-to-ceiling mirrors reflect the arrangement of colorful gowns and bolts of fabrics displayed neatly around the room. There's the faint scent of warm cinnamon that has me inhaling deeply as I try and knock off the snow that's clumped to my boots.

Edith Calloway and her perfectly curled blonde hair is already spinning in front of one of the tall mirrors ogling her own reflection. I would too if I was that pretty. She doesn't even notice when Collette turns away from her and welcomes us to her shop with a deep curtsey and a wide smile.

"Looking for something special for Yule?" Collette asks. Fine wrinkles appear at the edge of her sparkling green eyes, and her pointed ears stick out through the mass of stretched curls that fan out around her head. Her coral gown seems fitting in a room filled with so much pink and is a nice contrast to her deep brown skin.

"Yes, we're in need of a dress for Miss Weatherwood. You can charge it to my family's account," Malcom says quietly, pinning the modiste with a look that says this information stays between us.

"Of course, Mr. Black. If you'll follow me, Miss Weatherwood." She points to the back of the room where a space is curtained off.

Fingers much too warm for having been bare in the winter weather moments ago, wrap around my wrist slowing me. "I'll be back in a few hours to get you."

"No, you will not." I latch onto him, clutching the arm of his coat. "You're the one who said I should come here. You'll stay."

"Poesy, it's a dress fitting. You don't need me."

"I need you to tell me what looks best on me. What you think will catch Cassius' attention."

I swear his eye twitches, but he slowly uncurls his fingers from my wrist and straightens the cuff of his jacket. "Fine."

Being the true professional that she is, even though the modiste must think we're both out of our minds, she only politely smiles and offers Malcom a seat where he'll have a great view of the gowns I try on. She then ushers me behind a curtain. Even muffled with a layer of fabric between us, I can hear Malcom sigh. *Poor little baby.* Except I do cringe a bit into the mirror I'm facing when I hear Edith exclaim as she sees Malcom.

"Oh goodness, hi!" There's pitter patter of her probably very small and perfect feet as she scampers over to him. "It's soooo nice to see you again."

Sooooooo nice to see you. I mime the words back at myself in the mirror, my lips curling.

"Do you like this dress? Isn't this color perfect for me?"

I shove my finger into my mouth, pretending to get sick, only for the curtains to be pulled back and Collette to stroll inside with several dresses ready for me to try on. With my pulse racing and the feeling of getting caught coursing through me, my hands fall to my sides. In the time the curtain is pulled back, I get a small peek at Malcom smirking down at Edith.

You know what. They deserve each other.

And I deserve Cassius.

Then the curtain is tugged closed again, and

each ring holding it on the bar overhead hisses with the movement. Now it's just me and Collette. And several dresses I cannot afford.

"Let's get you into this one first; I think this would look darling on your figure." Collette holds a green dress up to herself so I can get a good look at it. The neckline is fairly modest, the skirt a gentle A-line that parts to reveal slivers of shimmering fabric that reminds me of dew-covered grass in the morning. She proceeds to undo the bindings of the dress I'd worn here and tugs the material up and over my head. One second, I'm inhaling fabric and the next I'm taking down a gulp of fresh air before she's forcing the new gown over my head.

Immediately, I notice a difference in the quality of the material. The fabric moves like flowing water around my body, a silkiness that is only comparable to the golden dress Malcom had gifted me. Is this the same modiste who owed him a favor?

"See, beautiful." She faces me toward the mirror, tucking my black bangs behind my ears as best she can. "Would you like to go show your...*friend*?"

"I suppose," I whisper. Already I feel crimson rising into my chest. Collette pushes back the curtain like she's revealing a massive surprise to the room beyond.

Malcom's lounged back in his seat. He turns to look at me, turning back to Edith only to glance back at me again. A double-take must be a good sign.

Edith pauses her admiring looks in the mirror and spins toward me. The red gown fitted against her perfectly curvy body fans out around her with the movement. "What do you think?"

I look from Malcom back to Edith. "Hi, Edith! I didn't realize you were going to be here today." Malcom raises a brow. "You look absolutely breathtaking. That is the *perfect* color on you."

And I wish I was lying. I wish I had a reason to not like the woman, but she truly is pretty and as far as I've known her to be, kind enough. I almost feel bad for mocking her.

"It's truly so nice to see you again. You know Cassius had nothing but wonderful things to say about you yesterday and I so dearly wanted to get to know you better. Now here you are. It's like fate." Edith walks forward with an air of confidence I've never mastered and wraps me up in her arms. The perfume lingering on her skin, soft and sweet like vanilla, complements the cinnamon scent of the shop. She's beautiful *and* she smells amazing. No wonder Malcom gets all weird when she's around. Even I could eat her right up.

"That sounds lovely," I purr. "Do you have any shopping to do? I've still got to purchase the last few gifts for my sister and father for Yule. We could have a little shopping day together." I don't mention that they're the only gifts I'm buying for my family.

"Most of my shopping is done, but I'm sure a little extra wouldn't hurt. That sounds great. Oh!" She pauses finally getting a good look at me. "This dress is great. Come show it off."

Her touch is light as a feather. Supple soft skin caresses my hand, guiding me more than anything else. The crystals sewn onto her dress sparkle under the light as she moves. Edith takes a step to the side giving me a full view of myself in the mirror. Malcom's eyes lock on mine for a heartbeat before he looks down at his hands, clasped in his lap.

Collette hovers around us too, fanning out the skirts and fixing our sleeves so they sit just right. "What a pair of beautiful young ladies I have in my shop today," she murmurs as she fusses.

"What do you think, Malcom?" Edith juts her chin in his direction.

"Looks fine."

Fine. Wow, what a compliment.

"Don't mind him. He's as cranky as they come." Her smile turns a bit sanguine.

"How do you feel in it?" Collette pushes.

"Good." I smooth my hands down the front, tilting my head one way and then the next. Here in this shop, surrounded by gowns, and magic blessed fairies, I feel like my old self. I nearly look like her too. Only I didn't used to have such hollow-looking eyes with dark bags underneath and I had perhaps more meat on my bones too. Once I belonged here, now I feel...odd.

Edith clicks her tongue. "But you don't love it."

"Let's try another!" Collette declares before I've even said anything more.

And four dresses later and lots of pleasant and polite chit-chat between myself and Edith, I step out in a lavender gown that Edith herself picked out. She'd stated that she thought the color would look perfect with my skin tone. Now that I'm looking at myself, feeling as though I'm glowing, she might be very right. It's possible that I like the girl. Malcom, however, has sunken down in his chair so much so that I wonder if he's cutting off some of the airflow with how his head is cocked. He doesn't even twitch as I stand there in front of the room.

"Wow," Edith whispers, "This has to be the one."

Malcom cracks an eye. His throat bobs once. Then he promptly closes his eyes again.

Gingerly, I touch the delicate lavender lace that frames the neckline of the dress. The full sleeves sparkle with clear crystals along the edges, as I turn one way and then the next trying to see myself from all angles. Fine material falls down my body, slimming me. Edith has good taste in gowns.

"This is the one." I nod.

"Perfect." Malcom groans, stretching and glancing behind him to the shop windows. The sun has made its way to the horizon the sky painted in pretty pinks and purples. "It's getting dark, so I need to get you home anyway." He turns back, finally getting an actual look at me, and freezes.

"What?" I demand more than ask. The way he's looking at me, I fear that the mirror in front of me is playing tricks. Maybe I'm secretly hideous and I don't know it.

His throat bobs. "Sorry, nothing. I hadn't gotten a good look at you in that dress yet. It's lovely." He gives a deep bow to the modiste. "Collette you've done a wonderful job per usual."

"It is not my dress," she tuts, "but the wearer."

"You look stunning, Sonnet." Edith steps forward giving my arms a little squeeze. "I must be on my way too. Cassius and Father will be wondering what's taken me so long."

I spin toward her, the dress twisting around my legs with the movement. Edith's hands are soft and warm as I take them gently in mine. "Truly, thank you for making this experience so wonderful."

"Anything for a friend." Her grip tightens momentarily in mine. "And we are new friends, yes?"

"Yes." I agree. Warmth floods my chest. We'd come here for a dress and to get close to Edith and I've successfully done both. Guilt is quick to follow, though, darkening the newfound warmth. I didn't genuinely seek out her friendship; I've used her to get an invitation for the ball. We're new friends, and I quite like Edith now that I've spent time with her, but I've tainted our friendship, and she doesn't even know it.

It's that haunting thought that lingers in my mind as I change back into my own clothing and leave the shop with Malcom. Behind us, Collette flips the shop sign to closed and pulls the curtains tight.

"I'll walk you home," Malcom says, flipping the collar of his coat up to shield himself from the wind. "Are you cold?"

I grip the edges of my cloak, holding it close. "It's gotten a bit chillier out, hasn't it?"

He holds out his hand, palm up. I stare down at it.

"Take my hand, Poesy." His voice is tender and gentle. My eyes dance between his extended hand and his face. A slight smile tilts his lips, a playful light flickering in his eyes. "I don't bite," he continues, "unless you want me to."

My stomach flips. Do I want him to? Yes. No. Oh goodness.

This is a bad idea, I think even as I place my hand in his. *A very bad idea.*

SONNET

Malcom's magic is a swirling, heated, thing that surges through our cradled palms and up into my arm to the rest of my body. The cloak is useless with his magic keeping away the chill. I let loose the edges to let them flap at my sides, content with my hand in his.

The lights of Daydale's Main Street are distant behind us. Only the moon and the stars above light our path forward as we near the Bitten Woods. The steady crunch of our footfalls over the compacted snow and the thump of my heart in my chest is the rhythm to which we move into the tree line. Small pink blossoms open at our nearness. A bud stretches toward us opening to flash shiny yellow fangs. Its teeth graze Malcom's coat before I pull him toward me. Our shoulders bump together, and I breathe out a chuckle.

"This was a successful trip. Sounds as if you and Edith were fast friends," Malcom says, tipping his head toward me.

I'd wring my hands together if I was willing to give up Malcom's warmth. But I'm not. So instead, I shrug. "Do you think it's enough? Edith seems kind, but Cassius barely remembers I exist unless I'm standing right in front of him. Is Edith's friendship enough to get me into the Yuletide Ball? Is your friendship enough?" Questions claw their way out of my throat falling from my lips in one rapid surge.

One of Malcom's blond brows raises. "Are we *friends*?"

"Are we?" I hold up our intertwined hands.

"This is just proof that I'm a gentleman who won't let you freeze out here."

"Oh."

And here I thought we were maybe more than two people bonded by a blood oath. Silly me.

"It's enough. Cassius is very blasé with all the women in his life; you're no exception. Edith, though, she's as authentic as they come. If she says you're her friend, then you are. Don't doubt yourself so much." His thumb strokes once against mine and my steps falter.

Righting myself, I take a slow inhale. Cold winter air fills my chest, quickly warmed. "You think so?"

"Yes."

"Cassius has said some very sweet things, and he's concerned that you and I could be something, so I think that's a good sign. Surely, he's only asking because he wants to pursue something with me. Right?" His eyes narrow but he doesn't answer so I continue talking. "He's told me that he finds me beautiful." I leave out the parts about how he touched me, his fingers dancing across my features as he spoke.

Malcom slows, his body turning toward me ever so slightly. "You do know he's just saying those things. He doesn't actually mean them."

I stop completely. "What? Why would you say that?"

"Because it's true, Poesy. Cassius is a serial flatterer. He gives out compliments freely but rarely does he mean them. Trust me, if you heard him speak about women in private you wouldn't be so proud of his flowered language."

A deep ache grows in my chest. Am I truly that naive? Am I so unattractive that Malcom must correct me and let me know that no one could ever sincerely mean it when they say I'm beautiful?

I rip my hand out of his. Bitter cold floods

back into me. Every brush of the breeze is like daggers to my skin instead of the gentle graze of air. "Wow, Malcom, two insults in less than five minutes. I'd think it would be a record for you, but I know better. You're wicked and mean. I'm sure you've said crueler things, but this still hurts." Quickening my pace, I leave him several feet behind me.

"What do you mean? I'm just being honest. I didn't mean to offend you." The thump of his footfalls trail behind me. "Poesy. Stop. It's dangerous out in these woods."

"You've never cared about my safety before. I walk through these woods alone all the time. How do you think I get home from work, Malcom? And you know more than anyone else that I'm not some damsel in distress. I don't need you to be a *gentleman*."

Heavy and hot, his hand falls on my shoulder slowing me, but I dodge out of his grip. "I didn't mean that we aren't friends, and I never said you weren't attractive."

"Both those things were implied"

"Not intentionally."

"So only in your subconscious do you think that I'm too ugly to be with Cassius and that we could never in a million years be friends."

"No—"

"How you have any friends is beyond me," I

snarl, spinning around to face him. Pink has crept into his cheeks; his dark eyes are wide and glimmering with something I don't recognize in him. Worry? Guilt?

"Can I speak?" He sighs.

I wave my hand before crossing my arms over my chest and waiting. "Please do."

"You are argumentative and a pain in my ass, but we are friends. If we weren't I wouldn't have sat through that dress fitting today. You care fiercely about those you love. You shoulder the responsibility of your family as if it weighs nothing, and you're strong enough to fight off a grown man in the woods. You are special, Poesy. Trust that I do care for you as much as my withered black heart can. I never meant that you aren't beautiful. It's just that Cassius would tell any woman that whether he thinks it or not. You are stunning. Truly the most beautiful creature I've ever encountered. Fuck..." He runs his hands through his hair. "For a moment, in that gown earlier, my heart stopped working. You're an angel here on earth and I can't believe for even a moment that I get the privilege to even look in your direction. Cassius does not deserve you. No one in this forsaken court does."

Any sort of rebuttal I'd started to build in my head dissolves in an instant. Silence envelopes us as I struggle to hold the intensity of his stare. My anger deflates.

"Say something," he whispers, shuffling closer. Somewhere in the woods a flower snaps its jaw closed and an owl hoots.

What can I say to...to *that*?

Slowly, as if he's afraid to spook me, he brings a hand up to cup my cheek. His warmth immediately floods my body and I almost sag in relief. He grazes his thumb over my bottom lip, eyes darting down to my mouth. He leans closer and I stiffen.

This can't be happening. Not with Malcom. No. This is all for Cassius. I'm supposed to get my invitation, and I want Cassius to be my date. I want Cassius. Right? Doubt creeps in as I stare up at Malcom's face wondering what it would be like to let him kiss me now. What would it be like if he took me to his bed? How would those large hands feel trailing up my body? Would we love as fiercely as we fight?

He's close enough now that I can smell the chocolate he'd eaten at Collette's on his breath. I want to taste it on his tongue. The tip of his nose caresses mine and his eyes flutter closed, but I can't bring myself to close my eyes. We're so close to the holiday. I've nearly gotten what I want. And the deal clearly says that he can't be my date. No. We're just friends.

I put my hand on his chest, pushing gently. His eyes flutter open and he straightens.

"Thank you for clarifying, Malcom." I laugh a little. "You've said the meanest and nicest things you've spoken to me all in one night."

His following chuckle is dry. One by one his fingers curl into his palm from that one outstretched hand. A tulip turns in our direction snapping toward us. We step together to avoid it, and I hate and love the nearness of our bodies.

"Watch out, they'll take a bite out of your jacket." I smile.

"I can't believe you walk these woods alone."

"I know." I slip my hand back into his, a sign of friendship. "Anyone could get robbed out here by gambling fairy men who know not what to do with their debts."

SONNET

The next evening the sky is clouded over, casting the way through the Bitten Woods in darkness. I trail along my path from memory alone, feeling more than seeing the small snowflakes that drift down around me. Already, I can smell the woods. Familiar and mundane, the scent of florals and pine lingers even at this distance.

I find the kink in my neck from hunching over Dr. Lowen's papers and rub gingerly. The blisters I've garnered from my walk are well on their way to healing. Something I can be thankful for.

Gray clouds shift ever so slightly allowing a sliver of the moon to peek out. Ahead of me, the tree line appears. So does the shape of a man. I squint, clutching my bag with my book in it like the weapon I know it to be. Moonlight dances over white-blond hair and dark eyes and my body relaxes. Malcom. His hands are tucked into his pockets, his double coat layers making his form appear bulkier.

"I almost hit you with my bag again!" I call out as he pulls himself away from the tree he'd been leaning against.

"That won't be necessary this time."

Huffing a laugh, we fall in step next to each other, heading toward my home. "What are you doing here? There should be no reason to rob me unless you already gambled away that ring again." My fingers move on their own accord to stroke the silver circle burned into my palm.

"I couldn't relax thinking about you walking home in the woods alone again." His voice drops to a whisper. "There are all sorts of criminals out here."

"You're the first and only criminal I've run into on my walks home for the last six months. I promise I'm safe."

His body is tense as he walks next to me. "Then you can merely enjoy my company."

This feels like he's waving a white flag, as though for once we can lay down our weapons and just exist. It's an offer I'll happily take, even if only because I enjoy his presence when he's not making me go out of my mind.

"Are you cold?" He offers me his hand.

The memory of his magic running through my body has been one that's lingered. Just as the reminder of the line we nearly crossed has. I've replayed that night over and over in my mind. Had he leaned in to kiss me? Am I reading too much into it? It feels safer to keep my hand to myself. It's not fair to me or to Cassius who's already admitted to wanting to court me. Not that he's called on me or so much as sent a letter.

With a shake of my head, I tuck my hands back inside my cloak. *Great, now I'm a thief and a liar.*

"I should apologize." His voice is gruff. Though I'm sure saying I'm sorry is not something he's very good at. "Again." His gaze, a lighter caramel shade tonight, flicks to mine before he watches the trail in front of us once more. "I said something I shouldn't have the other day. And you're right, Cassius could very well truly be interested in you. He didn't say anything that isn't true."

"You've already apologized. I accepted. Everything can go back to how it was," I say with a firm nod. Everything will be easier if we go back to being two people who've made a deal and nothing more. We can be friends, I suppose, but nothing more. We can't toe this line together. Not when all I've desired is so damn close.

"Back to how it was." His chin dips in agreement, his words soft, distant even.

Though as soon I get a glimmer of this quiet, unsure version of himself, it's gone. He spins in the snow and dirt, walking backward several paces ahead, and looks down at me. "So what's with the Yuletide List anyway?"

"What do you mean?"

"Why make it?"

"To have the best holiday ever." To fill the gaping hole of hurt that is the loss of my mother. To make sure that Merry smiles this holiday instead of crying as she remembers everything we've lost. And to show Father that we'll be okay. That we are okay.

"Your holiday will only be the best if you kiss someone under the mistletoe?" He smirks and the contemplative look in his eyes is replaced with mischief.

Okay, so maybe that one is just for me. Maybe I'm selfish and want to feel something other than sorrow. Something more than everyday boredom and stress. Maybe I want to feel loved. Cherished, even. Something. *Anything*.

"Kissing under the mistletoe is perhaps the oldest tradition in the holiday rule book. I intend to do all the holiday things and take advantage of every ounce of holiday magic I can." I lift my chin, showcasing my determination.

"Is that a real book, Poesy?"

"No, but everyone knows that. I don't need a book to tell me. Holiday magic is the only magic I might ever experience."

"I wondered if you had some sort of ability other than proving to be very capable of getting under my skin." He winks and I'm reminded of why exactly it is so tempting to let him get so close. Malcom Black is beautiful.

"No magic here. My mother was able to see glimmers of the future. She told fortunes and read palms. No one else in my family has any power. Hence why we were forced from our home in Matcher's Square."

"You lived on Matcher's?"

I hum a little to myself. "For years. Most of my life really. Until Mother passed and the king formally kicked us off the land to give to another family who does have magic. I think the Raths live there now." They are not as high born as Mother had been, but they show promise with their ability to change the color of any object with one touch. It's a party trick that the son and daughter often pull out, turning other fairies lovely shades of purple or blue. To change the subject, I ask, "Who are you going to kiss under the mistletoe? Edith?"

Malcom wrinkles his nose. Turning on his toe he ends up at my side again. "Edith is lovely, but I only ever flirt with her to piss off Cassius. Every time we speak, I'm practically bored to tears. She's too proper. Nice to look at, though."

"How about Geraldine? Or Tilly?" Both women I'd met, if only briefly, during the Hollis' event. The sisters, fraternal twins, are tall ethereal-looking creatures. Their skin glows like moonlight. Their hair, one a brilliant shade of red and the other onyx, practically sparkles.

"Been there. Done that." Malcom shrugs before wagging his eyebrows. "What about Trudy?"

"You stay away from her, Malcom Black." I swat at him, laughing as he dodges and jogs ahead breaking out of the treeline and onto the street where my house is. The lingering shame of him seeing the place I live is a ghost that haunts me as I chase after him, but he's come all this way and it's not like he doesn't already know where I live. "Don't you dare touch my friend. She doesn't need someone like you tainting her reputation."

"Oh, but I see the way she looks at me. I wonder what her kiss tastes like..." He taps a finger against his chin.

"You don't need to wonder anything when it comes to Trudy Hollis, but..." I look up at him. "I bet she tastes like that cherry balm she likes to put on her lips. I've used it before, it's rather nice." A slow smile spreads across his face as though he's imagining it now. Acid burns at the back of my throat knowing he's thinking of kissing her. "Do all men think about the taste of a woman's kiss?" I ponder out loud as my home comes into clear view.

The light blue shutters hang crooked next to the two windows at the front of the house. It's an odd shade when compared to the brown-orange of the front door. Eventually, I do plan on painting them so everything matches. Sadly, I've not had time between work and all this holiday prep. The gate on the rusting three-foot-tall iron fencing that frames our property stands ajar. The lock on it has never really worked right. What little garden there might have once been or possibly could exist is mostly a patch of unused dirt on the side of the house. All these things feel glaringly painful to look at as I approach with Malcom at my side.

"More than you'd think," Malcom confirms my earlier question.

"This is me." I slow and wave a hand at the pathetic excuse of property we live on.

His eyes don't bother to leave my face to look at my home. Malcom holds my attention, placing a hand on the iron gate and pushing it open.

"Want to know what I think your kiss would taste like?"

I roll my eyes trying not to let on how badly I want to know as I reach toward our mailbox, fixed to one side of the gate. "Enlighten me."

"Sugar plums. Sweet but tart. It would stain too, you know. A kiss from you would change a man's soul. I hope to see if after this holiday Cassius is a different man."

My hands tremble at the images his words produce. Everything I want is so close. Everything we're working for is within my grasp. I can do this. We can do this. We'll save this holiday season yet.

A thick envelope sits inside our mailbox. I pull the letter out, noticing the weight of the letter. "You and me both," I answer, flipping it over to see my name scrolled across the front. In the top left a return address is listed. For. The. Calloways.

Whatever Malcom says next, I don't even hear as my head starts buzzing with excitement. I tear through the parchment, dropping the envelope, and reading the fanciful writing that loops across the page.

You are cordially invited to the

Yuletide Ball

An evening of music, drinks, and dancing, hosted by the
Calloway Family.

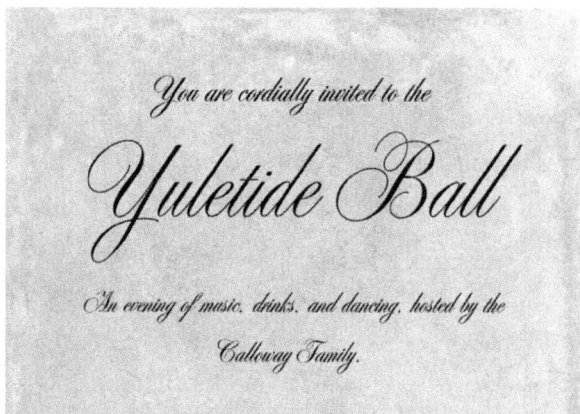

A squeal born of unbridled excitement jumps right out of me. I swear my body is levitating. An invitation!! I've gotten us an invitation to the Yuletide Ball! With Malcom's help of course. Suddenly, everything seems worth it.

"Good news?" His question comes from over my shoulder as he leans down to read.

In my excitement, I twist into his arms, wrapping myself around him like a vine growing up a tree trunk, and pull back to plant a sloppy kiss right on his lips. First, I notice the soft shape of his mouth on mine, then the way he opens against me as if asking for more.

Then I realize what I've done.

I pull myself back, sucking in a breath.

"I'm so sorry," I whisper.

Malcom blinks then straightens his shoulders as his throat bobs before he gives a nervous chuckle. Red creeps up into his cheeks. His fingers rise to brush against his lips. "As I guessed. Sugar plums." He grins, though it's without the enthusiasm he'd had before.

I know my face must be a dark stain of crimson as heat hurtles through my body. "Thank you for walking me home. I must tell my family." I wave the letter around for good measure.

Yes, hello, remember this awesome invitation. Forget about that kiss. It was only done as one friend to another. Out of excitement. Nothing more.

We've drawn our boundaries. If only we could learn to stick to them.

"Um, yes, of course. I'll be waiting for you at the woods again tomorrow. Er—" He gives an awkward wave. "Have a good night." With that, he turns back the way we came, but I don't watch him for long before I turn to sprint into the house.

Sugar plums, huh?

Malcom

Behind closed doors, men become terrible creatures. I know this not only because often *I* am terrible, but because in the gentlemen's club known as Rowdy's, I get to witness this phenomenon every week. With not a woman in sight, men become beasts. Drinks flow and tongues loosen. Every hideous thought they've ever conjured in their minds tumbles from their lips encouraged by every bastard at their side.

Rowdy's has been a usual haunt for me for a couple of years now. The creaking floorboards, faded jade wallpaper, the warm yellow light of the roaring fire and lit sconces, and the polished but occasionally wobbly tables are as familiar as the back of my own hand. Though recently, I've not had the time nor the mind to find myself here, today requires a drink. A stiff one at that.

Setting five gold coins on the bartop, I point a finger at the High Fae liquor held on the top shelf. For the steep price of five coins, to cover the cost and the hardship of getting it to the lesser fairy territories, I've reserved the drink for special occasions. Today is very *special*. Special in the way that I want to drown in the nearest river. Or in the way that I want to bury myself under a pile of blankets in my bed and never get back up.

Because I can still feel the fullness of Sonnet's lips pressed to mine. I can still taste that sweet yet tart sugar plum flavor as though she's still at the tip of my tongue, opening for me.

And as if the universe doesn't already hate me enough, Cassius slaps a hand against the counter and whistles as my drink is poured and placed before me. I don't turn to look at him. I don't focus on anything except the coldness of the glass against my palm and the burn of the liquor as it goes down my throat. My body warms a fraction.

"Drinking the good stuff tonight, eh?" Cassius leans back on the countertop, elbows holding him up as he gazes with hooded eyes at the rest of the room.

I set the now empty glass down against the counter with an audible thud. Coins jingle together in my deep pocket as I dig around to gather five more. The bartender's eyes widen as he watches me drop the payment for another drink between us. I hardly have to lift a finger before he's moving to pour the next glass.

"Hello, Cassius," I finally mumble watching the dark liquor rise in my glass.

"What has you all sour-looking?" He tips his head toward me, golden hair falling in front of his red-rimmed eyes.

"Same old shit."

"You don't need to be here tonight then. You need to go down to Beg and Barter." A smug smirk darkens his typically bright features.

Ah, Beg and Barter. The local whorehouse. He thinks I need to crawl into bed with a woman. While the release might be nice, I know I'd leave feeling worse. Feeling slimy and gross. Feeling even more undeserving of everything I'm wanting right now.

"I think I need some peace and quiet." I give a subtle nod to tell the man to leave me alone but if Cassius catches the subtlety, he ignores it. When the glass is filled and pushed toward me, I snatch it up, inhaling the bitter scent, and take a large gulp. This glass I'll savor. And if I'm lucky my body and mind will go numb.

"Come now, Black." His large palm curls over my shoulder and steers me away from the counter only for us to end up at a table with four others seated around it, including my brother. I recognize these men who run in the same circles as me, but none I would readily call a friend. A table full of acquaintances can't be trusted for none know me well enough to have reason not to cause harm. Especially as a fairy.

Eames, though, is a welcome sight. He rubs a hand against his stubble-lined jaw and watches me. "Brother." He lifts his glass.

I return the salute, not quite able to muster a real smile, and his eyes become two narrowed slits.

The chair I pull away from the table squeals against the floorboards and groans as I lower my weight into it. Our shared table is worn from years of use, smooth under my arm as I set my drink down. More than one man eyes the glass, noticing the pricy purchase. Normally, I'd love to flaunt my wealth before them, to remind them why the Blacks are one of the most prominent families here. Not today. Today it feels wrong. Because where I see the excess of my money, my mind conjures up images of Sonnet's simple home and visions of her bright red cheeks as she walks herself to and from her work.

Never in my life have I needed to walk the distances she does for her family, nor have I hardly had to work. My father's role in the Court of Frost is one that I'll take over and I've been trained to do as such, but until then my days have been filled with studies, swordsmanship, and messing around with other privileged fucks. My life is great. Easy even. So why does everything feel so very wrong right now?

I know why. I want that easiness for Sonnet and her family. And I don't want to be having feelings for anyone right now—especially the woman I'm trying to set up with Cassius. Courting, marriage, and women outside of quick release are not something I was planning on dealing with for several more years. Then I met Sonnet. And I can't get the women out of my damn head. I'll be carrying on with my day only to suddenly be thinking about the way she laughs or how powerful her right hook is. Then we stole the ring...and it knew her, it called to her, called to us. Only I made a blood oath not to be her date. Not to be her kiss under the mistletoe. Not to be the man who makes this holiday special for her.

Simply, I am the man who tries to rob women in the dead of night to right my wrongs. I'm the man who gambles and is happy to rot away in my role, uncaring for others. I'm not Cassius. I don't charm the masses or host balls. I host parties that end up dissolving into orgies and riots.

"Invitations went out. I expect you all to be in attendance." Cassius' lazy smile feels like someone is shoving nine-inch nails directly into my chest. I take another sip of my drink.

"Oh, we'll be there," Carter Damascus, the son of the man who owns Daydale's private school, raises his glass and answers for the group.

"All work will be well worth it when I finally get to take my little investment home for the night," Cassius continues with a wag of his brows.

"Ah, the Weatherwood girl you've been entertaining?" Dean Marsh circles a finger around his glass.

My gaze snaps to Cassius. Eames' gaze stays locked on me. "Sonnet?" Her name is rough on my tongue, and I have to clear my throat.

"Right..." Cassius nods. "I forgot you're the reason we even met. She's quite infatuated with me, you know? The way she stares at me, I know she is *interested*."

"Mmmm." I hum my regrettable agreement taking another desperate drink. A creeping desire for apathy spreads through me along with the warmth fueled by the Fae liquor. I don't want to care about what Cassius may or may not think of Sonnet or what he plans to do with her.

"I thought she had a thing for Malcom," Eames interjects earning himself a glare from me.

"Not at all," I bite out.

"It wouldn't really be competition anyway." Cassius laughs and claps me on the back again.

Maybe coming here was a bad idea.

I shrug away from his touch well aware of the magic pulsing through me as my annoyance grows.

"We're all gambling men here." Carter leans forward, sliding a coin to the center of the table. "Shall we bet on the likelihood that Cassius here gets his wick wet? Do we think his investment will pay off with lifted skirts?"

The question causes the men to all laugh and dig into their pockets. Fury simmers under my flesh only weakly held off by my growing numbness. I shift in my seat trying to let my drink do its work and to ignore the terribly uncomfortable feeling.

"You're not interested in the girl?" Eames asks, not yet moving for his coin.

"Just friends." And I hate it.

"I'll take that bet and raise you." Dean slaps two coins down. "I bet he keeps her wine glass full and by the end of the night she'll be too drunk to even notice he's got her out of her gown."

My attention drills into the table. Don't react. Don't fucking react. Every breath has to make its way through my tightening throat and the rising suffocating feeling of rage. My body stills as Cassius drops his buy-in to the bet. The coins spin against the wood again and again and again before stopping with a definitive *clink* that I feel deep in my very soul.

"I bet I won't need to get her drunk. I bet before the party even ends I'll be able to get her to leave without a chaperone and she'll be crying my name out within the hour."

Something in my chest snaps right in half.

"What about you, Black?" Carter tips his chin in my direction.

"I've recently given up on gambling," I manage to say.

Eames chokes on the sip he's taking, looking at me as though I've grown another head.

It's Cassius who chuckles and nudges me with his elbow. "I never thought I'd see the day that Malcom Black gives up gambling. No bother really, I'll be happy to take the rest of your money though. The girl practically lives in a shack for crying out loud, she'll be eager to please me."

"Oh, save me, Cassius, save me," Dean mimics in a feminine voice.

"I don't particularly think she'll be eager to do anything for you," I snap.

"If you feel so strongly, you can put some of that money behind it. Or did you spend it all on your two drinks?" Carter laughs, mocking me.

Anger wraps its tainted, fire-hot fingers between every vertebra in my spine. I lean back into my seat. "Sonnet isn't some weak-kneed maiden fawning over you."

She's trying to make the loss of her parent hurt a little less. She's working within the standards and rules society has forced upon her. Sonnet Weatherwood would never give herself to Cassius. Not without a courtship. Not without a wedding.

"We'll see, won't we?" Cassius touches a finger to every coin sitting at the center of the table. "She's a pretty little thing despite her lack of magic. If only she wasn't so pathetic. The only thing women like that are good for is choking on my length."

Dean and Carter nod as if Cassius didn't say the most disgusting thing I've ever heard in my life. And I've heard men speak of women in such terms all my life. Damn it all, I've spoken of women like this. But Sonnet...is different. Sonnet is *mine*.

No, she's not. I remind myself. She's not. She wants Cassius.

And would I want her if Cassius ruins her?

Yes. I'd still want her.

That answer alone terrifies me.

"Honestly, I should have bet that she'd give it up before then. She expected me to call on her and I haven't. I'd probably need to invite her out one time and I'd have her back pressed against the wall in no time."

"Would you shut it?" I shout, the words coming despite the effort I put into shoving them deep, deep down.

Eames sits forward in his seat, attention bouncing between Cassius and me.

"Are you jealous, Malcom?" Cassius sticks his lip out in a mock pout. "I've seen you running around with her yet you're nothing but a brother to her. Couldn't get it done, could you?"

A knock at my pride but that stings a lot less than them thinking she's some common whore. "I'm not jealous, but you don't know anything about her. I don't think she'll follow you anywhere."

"We'll see." He drums his fingers against the table, laughing again. The sound only fuels the fire inside of me. "I'll let you know how her cunt feels."

My chair clatters to the floor behind me as I jolt right out of my seat. His collar bunches in my palm as I yank him out of his chair. "Don't you fucking talk about her like that," I say through clenched teeth.

Eames is at my side, hand on my shoulder. "Let's take a breather. Go outside."

My grip tightens and I ignore Eames' plea for peace.

Cassius' body is tense, but he plucks at my fingers as though he has no care in the world, loosening my hold on his shirt. "It's just a joke."

"Is this a fucking joke?" My jacket strains with the movement as I pull my arm back and send my fist directly into his smug face. Someone shouts behind me. Probably my brother. Not that I care.

Cassius' head snaps back with the force of the hit. The blue of his eyes blazes as he realizes what happened. Dean and Carter are both out of their seats, but it does nothing to stop the ensuing fight as Cassius launches himself at me. We collide in a mess of limbs and jabs, knocking into Eames who stumbles backward and lands on his ass. Cassius' knuckles bust open my lip and make my teeth clack together. I send an elbow into his temple. He knocks the breath from my lungs.

Distantly I recognize the snap of wood as we throw ourselves at each other and trip over one of our chairs. There's shouting and cheering and all of it feels...good. Every blow I take is a punishment I deserve. It's better than the pain of stewing in my own mind.

It all ends quickly. Too quickly. Eames, Carter, and Dean finally get their wits about them enough to work together and pull us apart.

I taste the copper of my blood on my tongue as spit the excess onto the floor. Cassius touches a finger to the cut along his hairline, bleeding enough to drip down his face and onto his shirt. My jaw feels sore and my eye possibly swollen.

And Cassius laughs.

He laughs and pulls himself out of Carter's grip. "Damn, Black. If you're so interested in the woman, why don't you do something about it?"

Malcom

Sonnet's home is rougher when viewed in the sunshine of day instead of when it's swathed in the shadows of night. The shutters hang crooked and the roof looks as though it's seen better days. Around the yard the short iron gate is rusted in several places, leaving me to wonder what good the gate even does. There's a worn path to the door where grass doesn't grow and a withered wreath on the door.

I touch a finger to the gate, and it practically whistles as it opens. Tugging at the hem of my jacket, I make my way to her door. Apart from walking her home the other night, I've not ever been to her house. She's not wanted me to. Perhaps that says something of my appalling character that she's not trusted me enough. Not that I've given her reason to trust me yet. Today is the first step in the right direction. I'll warn her off Cassius, protect her reputation. Earn that trust.

Gods. Is this what it feels like to be decent? Ech. It's entirely uncomfortable and I'm not sure I like the feeling.

My knuckles rap against the door. Once. Twice. Three times. And I wait. Shifting from foot to foot, I let my gaze wander down to the compacted snow underfoot. Small impressions of her leather boots lead to and from the little home. Inhaling, slowly, I try to calm my rapidly beating heart.

The door cracks open, revealing an older, quite serious man that I quickly recognize as her father. My father has never answered the front door on his own that I'm aware of. My throat is scratchy and rough as I give the man a slight bow. "Mr. Weatherwood." I cough to clear my throat. "I'm not sure if you remember me, but my name is Malcom Black. Is Sonnet home?"

Bright green eyes search me from head to toe, lingering on my bruised jaw and scabbed lip. "Of course I remember you, Mr. Black. Long sword, double edge blade, weighted hilt with some of my best detailing work. An expensive piece. How could I forget?" Though his words are light and friendly, he doesn't smile. "Sonnet's getting ready for the day. I'll fetch her." He opens the door wider only to pause as he looks behind him into the home. "Er, we don't have a sitting room really, but you're welcome to...stand by the door."

"Happily." I offer him the same smile that's dazzled so many. Denver Weatherwood only stares at me a heartbeat longer before disappearing further into the home, unimpressed. *So, this is going terribly.* Stepping over the threshold, I'm hit with the sweet scent of baked goods. Greedily breathing it in, I close the door to lock out the cold, and carefully fold my hands in front of me.

Inside the home is not much better than the outside. The floorboards are curling at their ends making every step her father takes through the makeshift dining room and living space an announcement that echoes through the small space. Following the warm scent, I peer into the kitchen—which to my dismay is only a small oven and cabinet space shoved into one corner of the room. *That's* hardly a kitchen at all.

Merry stands frozen by the counter, a flour-covered apron wrapped around her body. The young girl's eyes are as wide as saucers, her lips parted in a perfect 'O.' My attention meets hers and she blinks so hard her entire face scrunches.

"Malcom?" she whispers before squealing and running toward me.

"Hello, Merry," I wheeze as she wraps her arms around me, squeezing me so tight I can hardly take my next breath.

"Have you come for Sonnet? Are you courting? You two would make the most beautiful couple. You could be her date to the Yuletide Ball! I'm sure you were invited but I nearly died when I saw that Sonnet had been invited too. She is so lucky. I wish I was old enough to attend. Also, what happened to your face? I hope that heals quickly because you look awful."

After a minute of nearly spine-breaking pressure, the girl finally lets me go. I roll my shoulders trying to regain what little composure I'd come here with. "We're not courting. I'm only here to speak with her." Then to change the subject and avoid addressing the wreck that is my face, I say, "You're, um, bread smells good." I point to what I assume is bread but really looks mostly like a deflated log in a dish.

"Sonnet's trying to teach me to cook. It's not going well. She is washing up because somehow I sifted more flour onto us than into the bowl."

"I'm sure with time you'll be a talented baker."

She flashes a daring smile that's far too similar to her sister's and shrugs. "Unless I marry into a magic-bearing family, I'll have to figure out how to cook, but I fear my future family might be eating more pancakes than bread because this adventure has not gone well."

"It can't be that bad." Then because I have no self-preservation skills, I point down to the 'bread.' "Let me try a bite."

Her dark brows rise at the same time a smile, as wicked as I've ever seen, darkens her face. She grabs a knife and carves out a slender slice. The knife moving through the bread sounds like she's attempting to cut through a piece of wood with a spoon. She plops the piece into my now outstretched palm. Somehow, it's spongy, dry, and crumbling all at once. I've never seen any food look so...sad.

"Go on," she encourages.

I lift the bread to my mouth, regretting my offer, as soon as it touches my lips.

"Do *not* eat that," Sonnet warns from some-where behind me.

"Too late," I say around expanding crumbs and a texture that reminds me of a fish fillet.

In a flash of dark hair, Sonnet hurries into the kitchen and snatches up a hand towel, shoving it into my face. "Spit it out before you get some sort of disease."

I'm thankful for the chance to get this rotting excuse for food out of my mouth but when I look at Merry's fallen face, I shake my head at Sonnet and force myself to chew and swallow. It grates down my throat, leaving it a little raw, as I smile.

"I think it's missing something but otherwise it's great," I lie straight through my teeth.

Merry beams, and something in the deep black hole that's supposed to be my heart twitches.

"You did not need to do that." Sonnet frowns. "She very well could have poisoned you."

"Merry? Never." Still, I choke on the words a bit, some of the bread stuck somewhere in my esophagus.

Denver Weatherwood steps into the kitchen eyeing the flat thing in the pan and promptly turns and walks away. Honestly, smart man.

"Can we talk?" I ask, dusting off the crumbs that now litter the front of my shirt.

"We'll be over, um, here." Her father ushers Merry to the back of the house, but the space is really one big room so there truly isn't very much privacy.

"Sure, of course." Sonnet waves me toward the front door and away from her family. Her entire body freezes as she gets a full look at me. "Malcom, what happened to you?" She reaches for my face, but I gently bat her hands away.

"Don't worry about me. I'm fine."

Sonnet's hair is down, her tresses waving gently around her face, slightly damp. Her dress is a plain baby blue thing, buttoned all the way up to her neck, hiding away her beautiful skin. She tucks her hair behind her ear, something I'm incredibly thankful for as my fingers itched to do it for her. Glaring up at me for a second, she finally crosses her arms over her chest and sighs.

"What are you doing here? Is everything okay?" Her voice lowers to a whisper.

I know she's tracing my jaw with her gaze, but I stare down trying to get the words out because any which way I'm going to sound like an ass. I keep my voice low like hers. "Don't go to the Yuletide Ball with Cassius."

A crease forms between her brows. "Well, he hasn't even asked me yet, but why wouldn't I? Isn't that what all this is for?" And the unspoken need for her to marry up for her family hovers like a ghost in our conversation.

"I'll find you another date. Someone better suited for you."

"I don't understand. Cassius and I suit just fine. Does this have to do with our conversation the other day? Why can't you accept that maybe he does care for me?"

"It doesn't. And he doesn't." It comes out harsh and louder than I intend. With a glance over my shoulder, I see her father and sister pretending to find a painting on their wall very interesting as they murmur to each other. Her dark lashes flutter as she stares at me. So softer, I say, "He doesn't."

"You don't know that. Why are you being like this?" She looks over at her family too, turning us away from them further.

"The bargain does not say that your date must be him. I got you your invitation. You had your fun at Trudy's party. You'll get your damn kiss."

"Who else is going to take me? There is hardly enough time for me to entertain someone else. And *I* like Cassius."

"Can't you trust me when I say that you need to stay away from him?" I step closer only to hear her father clear his throat forcing me to take a step right back.

"No. I need a reason. You need to give me a reason." Her eyes are wide, pleading with me.

"Pick someone else. Anyone else," I plead right back.

Please, Poesy, don't make me say it.

Her spine stiffens. "Malcom, I think you need to leave. This is silly. You don't even have a reason. It's all nonsense. And you come in here with your face like"—she gestures up at me—"like that, with no explanation. What am I supposed to think?"

"Swear you'll find someone else." I want to reach out and touch her as if that would convey how serious I am about this, but her father is right there, watching, so I keep my hands to myself.

"I'm not going to do that." She reaches for the door. "You're worrying me. Please go before you stress out my family over nothing."

Cold blows in through the now open door, I take a step to leave, but turn back at the last moment as the urgency to make her listen takes hold of me. "Sonnet, please, heed my advice."

Her eyes tick up to mine and narrow. "You never call me Sonnet." Her slender body leans into the door, blocking my view of her home, her family. "Can you just be honest and tell me what's going on?"

Pinching the bridge of my nose, I force myself to answer. "He's placing bets on what it would take to get you into his bed."

She sputters a laugh. Stops. Her smile falls. "You're funny."

"I'm not being funny, Sonnet."

"There you go. Saying my name again. Call me Poesy like you always do."

"Don't." I hold a finger up. "Don't change the subject."

Her shoulders droop. "How do you know he's placing bets? Shouldn't you of all people stay away from gambling?" She shivers and I can imagine that her wet hair isn't helping so I reach out and put a single finger against her hand.

"Because I was there. I heard him say it. I didn't make a bet on it, I swear, but others did. I'm trying to protect you."

"I don't need you to protect me, Malcom," she whispers, gently pushing my hand away from her. "We're just using each other to fulfill this blood oath. That's it. Remember? Don't start acting like you've suddenly grown a conscious or have something resembling a soul now."

I straighten and take a step back as she throws my own words and sentiments right back in my face. And I deserve that. I deserve all of this, really. Sonnet, however, doesn't. She doesn't deserve to have Cassius and his stupid friends mocking her, betting on her, belittling her.

"I'll see you at the Yuletide Ball, Malcom."

The door clicks shut.

SONNET

"Miss Weatherwood, did you get Mrs. Tribune on my schedule?"

Who? Oh, right. I give Dr. Lowen a nod before going right back to staring absently at all the papers on my desk that I should really be doing something with. The pile of notes he's given me that I need to file is growing taller by the second. He knows I'm hardly working today but hasn't done more than gently remind me of a thing or two.

My mind isn't here. It keeps wandering back to what Malcom said. He's made it clear that he doesn't like Cassius. He's also told me how he doesn't have a heart or a soul for that matter. Malcom enjoys being the villain. The criminal. So why would I trust him? He's just being cruel.

Mostly, though, I don't want it to be true.

Cassius Calloway is my dream. He's the solution to my family's problems. I chew on my lip.

And none of that explains what happened to his face? The bruise was yellowing, which means I was already seeing it in the nearly healed stage. Malcom had brushed it off and redirected the conversation back to Cassius and how I should have nothing to do with him. How he's protecting me. As if I've ever needed protection from anyone other than him. Hot anger surges up inside of me again.

How dare he come to my house like that? How dare he darken my doorstep with his hideous rumors while my family was right there?

Still, seeing him there, politely encouraging Merry, and then looking at me with such frantic worry did something to me. It softened me where I've been trying too hard to keep my walls built up. No matter how many times I've called Malcom a friend or something like a brother, he's not. Underneath it all, there are feelings. Horrible, vulnerable, scary feelings.

He'd had his chance though. I'd given him the opportunity, practically begged him to say something. If he cared for me, if perhaps he felt a bit how I feel, he could have used it as a reason for me not to go with Cassius. That's all it would have taken. Yet once again, I'm left reeling, feeling as though I'm the confused one.

I let my head drop onto the desk with a thud and groan against the papers. I wish my mother was here. More than ever, I need her hug. We wouldn't be in this situation if she was around and even if we were she would know what to do. She'd smile, probably even laugh about it, then point out the glaringly obvious solution. Only, without her, nothing feels quite so obvious. Life's a puzzle I've not figured out how to piece together yet. Or a better analogy would be to say that I'm a soggy misshapen piece that doesn't fit into the otherwise perfect puzzle anymore. I'd fit once upon a time.

The door to the office swings open. Footfalls shuffle in. I sit up and a paper stays attached to my forehead as I do. "Ugh." I pull the paper off. "Dr. Lowen is with another patient, right now. How can we—"

"Miss Weatherwood?" Cassius' brows furrow.

"Oh, Sonnet!" Edith cheers my name, leaning heavily into her brother's side. "I'm so glad you're here. I've hurt my ankle something awful and I don't want it to bother me during the ball. I'm hoping Dr. Lowen could work his magic on it."

This is...perfect.

I try to smooth down my likely frizzy hair and tuck the fallen strands back behind my ears.

I'd come into work looking about as hectic as I've been feeling. Now that the Calloways are standing in front of me I regret my decision not to take the extra time to look more presentable.

"Yes. He'll be right with you." I stand and point at the arrangement of chairs in front of my desk. Most of which are odd and end pieces gathered over the years and make the office look more like a wizard's hovel. Especially with Dr. Lowen's eclectic art and the stacks of medical and magical books taking up all available space. "Have a seat and rest in the meantime.

As such a gentleman should, Cassius walks his sister to a chair and gently lowers her into the seat. He takes a moment, murmuring to her, and hands her a book. She looks more like a child who he's trying to keep busy than the grown woman I'd met at the store. Edith catches my stare and smiles with a little shrug before leaning back in the seat and opening the book.

Then my attention slips further up. Up to the pretty blue eyes watching me with amusement. My body remembers the brush of his fingers and the weight of that very stare. I force my shoulders back, correcting my slumped posture.

Cassius strolls forward, casually but somehow still with purpose. He makes it look easy as he stalks me like I'm his prey. His willing prey because I want to be the object of his desire. I need to be. He thumbs the edge of my desk and then picks up the small oddly shaped bit of wood I use as a paperweight. It was my father's first wood carving project and was supposed to be a heart but mostly looks like a potato. Still, I love it and the effort he put into it.

"I didn't know you worked here." He sets my lumpy heart back down.

"A little something to keep me busy. I like being helpful," I answer, avoiding the part where I took this job because we so desperately need the coin.

"You've got"—he reaches between us, rubbing his thumb against my forehead—"a bit of ink here. Got it."

My face burns red hot. I've got ink on my face. Because of course I do. Might I go crawl under a rock now?

"Oh, thank you. Sorry, I don't typically put my head down during the day. I've just been quite busy and I'm a bit tired because of it."

"No need to apologize to me. It's cute." Half his mouth pulls up into a smile. "You've got such a big heart. I shouldn't be surprised to see you here helping the court."

Up close it's easier for me to get a good look at his features. Even from where I'm sitting I can see the yellow-brown of a bruise along his hairline and another along the bottom of his jaw almost hidden in a shadow. I squint up at him and rise out of my chair, reaching for but not touching his face.

"What happened?"

He snorts. "Ah, got caught in a tussle between two drunken fools. I figure Dr. Lowen could easily fix this while I'm in there with Edith." His smile spreads to the other half of his mouth. "Are you concerned about me, Miss Weatherwood?"

I let my hand fall, and I know I'm grinning like a fool up at him. "Yes, actually, I am."

For a second I'd wondered if it was Malcom and him that had fought but Cassius said it himself, he got between two drunks. Malcom and some other man, I suppose. More the reason not to trust Malcom. He's got to be wrong about Cassius.

Cassius leans in, lowering his voice. "You are too sweet to me, Miss Weatherwood."

"Please, call me Sonnet. None of these formalities. We are friends, are we not?" My cheeks warm further as a bit of hope seeps into my voice.

"Friends. Yes, *Sonnet*, I think we are." He touches my father's wooden carving again, making it rock against my desk, before looking at me from under his lashes. "Did you receive your invitation?"

"We did. My father is beyond grateful. I'll happily be attending." And checking off another item on my holiday list. Eeekkkk!

"Have you..." He spins the carving around in his hand and an expression that I've not seen dawns on the man. Cassius dares to look, well, bashful almost. "Have you considered a date?"

"A date?"

He nods, attention dancing between the paperweight and me.

"I don't currently have...a date, no." And I have to look away. This could be leading up to something exciting or this could potentially be the most embarrassing conversation of my life. Edith peers at us from over her book. When my attention snags on her she quickly looks back down, pressing her lips into a thin line to suppress the smile on her face.

"Good. I was wondering if you'd like to come as *my* date."

I swear my heart stops beating altogether. Air is trapped in my lungs as my brain races to process what he's said to me. I'll attend the Yule-tide Ball and I'll have a date. Not just any date... but the date. The most eligible bachelor in the Court of Frost. Some magic is truly at play here because my holiday dreams might be coming true.

Sucking in a breath, I force myself to answer, desperate to keep my nerves from making my voice break. I swallow once. Twice. My throat is still impossibly dry.

"I would love that," I say.

He knocks a knuckle against my desk and flashes a wide grin. "Perfect, I'll see you then."

"Oh, thank goodness." Edith snaps the book closed. "I've been waiting for him to ask. I can't wait for him to see your dress and we're going to have such a wonderful time. Our cooks will be making a rather large and impressive Yule log too. So do come hungry. Oh, and there will be mistletoe." Edith sings the last bit as Dr. Lowen escorts his last patient out.

"Be careful of too much kissing under the mistletoe," Dr. Lowen says with a wink. "That can cause all sorts of diseases and I'll be out of the office for the holiday. Now, Miss Weatherwood, can you please write up this list for Mr. Braman to pick up from the local witchery?" He sets his messily scrawled list in front of me.

"Of course." I sit myself back in my seat, even though my entire body is humming. Cassius is my date for the Yuletide Ball. I'll be attending with one of the *Calloways*. Me. And Malcom didn't even have to set it up. I've done it all by myself.

Dr. Lowen turns to Edith, eyes scanning her. "A hurt ankle? Come let's get you taken care of." He looks at Cassius. "You shouldn't be getting into brawls at this age, but at least it's a quick fix."

"Perfect." Cassius rubs his hands together. "I'll see you at the Ball, Sonnet."

In just a few short minutes, the office is empty and it's only me and my stupid grin. Malcom had no idea what he was talking about. Cassius has only been a gentleman, and he's done more to make this holiday special than even Malcom has.

This will be the best Yuletide of my life.

SONNET

Though winter is in full swing and my cloak is hardly enough against the brutal winds and evening air, my body is still warm. Every inch of my skin crawls with excitement. The Yuletide Ball is nearly here and not only am I going but Cassius is my date and there will indeed be mistletoe with plenty of opportunity to take advantage of it, I hope.

What might his lips on mine feel like? Will butterflies erupt in my stomach? Will he be a good kisser? Will I? Oh goodness...what if I'm a bad kisser? Should I practice? With whom though?

At the entrance to the Bitten Woods, Malcom stands huddled in his two jackets. He pulls away from a tree and strolls to my side in silence. I hadn't expected him to return, and though I don't mind it, after our conversation when he'd come to my house...well, I thought, surely, he wouldn't want to be near me at all. Still, he came. I smile as he falls into step beside me.

Together we walk in silence for several minutes before I turn to him. "You really don't have to walk me home every night."

Though Cassius had left the office as we were closing and the sun was setting, he didn't so much as offer to give me a ride home or to walk with me. We merely said our goodbyes and went on our merry ways. Meanwhile, I've called Malcom cruel and a liar and he's still shown up. Something turns dark and shameful in my stomach.

"I need to know that you're safe," is all he says, not even bothering to look my way. Though I do imagine it would be hard to turn his head with his scarves wrapped so tightly around his face.

"That is very kind," I whisper into the night. It's several very long, quiet, and frankly awkward minutes before either of us speaks again.

"How was work?"

"Good, actually. Very good." I adjust the strap of my bag, my book weighing it down enough that it's begun to dig into my shoulder. Malcom sees the movement, pauses, then takes the bag right off of me and slips it onto his shoulder. "Thank you." He nods. "Edith and Cassius came into the office today. He had a few bruises; looked worse than you actually."

I swear I see the hint of a smile at that, but Malcom doesn't respond. He just keeps walking.

"Said he broke up a couple of drunken fools fighting..."

"Did he now?" He rolls his eyes.

"Yes, and then he asked if I'd be his date to Yule."

Malcom stops. He turns his whole body to face me, though I'm a step ahead of him now. "What did you say?"

Up until this moment, I've been excited. Thrilled even. My plan is going perfectly and my dreams are coming true. Now, having to speak it to Malcom...everything feels wrong.

"I said, yes."

His eyes drift closed. His expression pained. Somehow I feel that in my chest too as though his pain has echoed inside of me. "Congratulations, Poesy. You're getting exactly what you wanted."

"I am." We start walking again.

"You know you're better than him right?" he asks, and I nearly trip over my own two feet. Then he continues. "You're better than me too. You're the best person I know, actually."

"I doubt that very much." I try to give him a slight smile but the movement is awkward and stiff. "I've no magic, no money, no status. If anything I might very well be as terrible as you because I'm only using him for my own personal gain. I *need* to see my family well again."

"You're better than all of us. You're kind, actually kind. You're brave and strong, despite not having any magic. Poesy, you're smart. And though I loathe to admit it, you might actually be funny too."

"Are you trying to butter me up for something? I'll not go sneaking off into someone's home again."

He shakes his head. "No. I think I'm retiring from my criminal ways. I only mean to say... don't let him talk you into anything you don't want to do. You're worth so much more than he even realizes. Don't forget it."

"Thank you, Malcom." I set my hand on his arm, feeling the heat traveling through his coats. "I promise if at any point I am uncomfortable I will excuse myself. I can take care of myself."

"I know you can. You've proven it." He tilts his head in my direction.

Maybe it's his words that have bolstered my spirit, or maybe I'm simply as brave as he thinks I am, but I clear my throat and pull him to a stop next to me. "Actually, I have a favor to ask of you."

"More favors? Should we take another blood oath?" He finally cracks a smile then.

"Absolutely, not. Who knows what wicked thing you'll get me into next..." I laugh, but the sound dies on my lips. "Would you kiss me?" Malcom stares at me, a crease forming between his brows. "As a friend, I mean."

"Kiss you? As a friend?"

"It's only that I've not been kissed many times in my life. Edith confirmed that there will be a mistletoe there. If I am to be kissed under a mistletoe then I would like to be kissed well. I fear that I am not a good kisser so I thought that I should practice. I can't exactly practice with anyone in my home or with Dr. Lowen." I suppress a shudder at the idea and push on. "Then I thought of you. My friend. Unless, you don't think we should?"

We probably shouldn't.

"No, I'm just surprised is all." He sucks his lower lip between his teeth for a moment, his eyes distant, lost in thought.

"You know, this was a bad idea. I take it back." I wave a hand, with the hope we can both forget everything I said. Stars dance in my vision as I squeeze my eyes tightly shut, trying to hold off the wave of embarrassment currently warming my skin.

"I'll kiss you."

"What?"

"For *practice*. I'll kiss you," Malcom repeats.

Butterflies take flight in my stomach. A wonderful and terrible shiver runs down my spine. All around us the woods seem to hold its breath. Even the trees feel as though they've leaned in to watch us. The flowers are still, their petals turned toward the clear sky.

"Really?" I ask.

"Really. Let me set a few things down and I'll be ready."

The best I can offer him is the smallest dip of my chin as I stand rooted in place. He carefully sets my bag down and shrugs out of one layer of his coats. Our breaths cloud the air between us. Slowly, he unwinds the scarf from around his neck and drops it at our feet.

Malcom closes the space between us. I blink rapidly trying not to be weird despite how close we are. His hand, smooth and hot, slides up my neck and into my hair. His thumb frames the side of my face.

"Oh, we're doing this," I breathe the words out.

"I did take an oath."

"Nowhere in the oath are you obligated to

kiss me." My eyelids flutter closed as his thumb grazes against my skin. Goosebumps rise along my flesh. I breathe in his musky scent, happily filling my lungs with the same air he's breathing.

"Nevertheless..."

If there's more to the sentence he never gets around it. Not that I care one bit as he brings his lips to mine. I've been kissed before, mostly childish pecks but every other kiss I've had pales in comparison to this. This is a damn kiss.

Malcom's other hand finds my waist, pulling me against him. His mouth is gentle at first, tentative almost as if he's asking permission to go further. I open to him, allowing him entrance as his tongue explores against mine. Delicious heat spreads to my core. I let him hold me as my knees go weak and I have to press my thighs together to appease the sensation rising up inside of me.

His lips move against mine, tasting, nipping, savoring. I'm clumsy in my effort to keep up with him, but he hums appreciatively so perhaps I'm not as bad as I thought. When I move my tongue to play against his, his grip on my waist tightens and he lets out a low groan. My toes curl in my boots at the sound. Suddenly, I want more of those little noises from him.

I let my hands wander up against his firm chest, then further around to the nape of his neck. Clinging to him and intertwining my fingers into his hair, I lose myself to the kiss. His kiss. His hand on my neck circles my throat, holding me hostage to the onslaught of his caress. He squeezes gently and my head is light. Not from lack of air but because I want him to do more. Touch me more.

I'm not sure who pulls away but when we finally part, I'm panting against his chest. He sucks down air as though he's been submerged under water and holds me as we stare at each other.

"That was good, uh, practice." He swallows, his touch loosening.

On shaking legs, I force myself to take a step back. "You've done that a time or two, huh?" My lips feel warm and swollen from the kiss.

"Kissing? Yes." He clears his throat. "You're pretty good. You don't really need much practice. If you do though, I'm around."

"Right." Though I'm not sure if I can do that again. I feel as though I'm a baby deer learning to walk for the first time. If Malcom ever gave me another kiss like that...well, he might very well have to carry me home. I've got the feeling my father would not be very amused at that sight either.

Malcom avoids eye contact as he gets back into his jacket and picks up my bag. Silently, we continue along the path until the woods come to an end and my home is in sight. Tension hangs in the air between us for those last few steps. One I can't quite name, or one I'm not sure I want to.

This was a mistake. Friends don't kiss. I shouldn't have asked. Because now all I want to do is have him take me into his arms again, carry me to his bed, and—

"Oh, I almost forgot." Malcom digs inside his pants pocket and pulls out a rectangular box. "Happy Yule, Sonnet."

I take it in hand. Velvet fabric covers the box, and I stroke a finger against it. "I didn't think you did Yule gifts?"

"Maybe I do now." He lifts a shoulder. "It matches your dress for the Yuletide Ball. If you don't like it you don't have to wear it. It belonged to some grandmother somewhere down the line, though, so if you don't like it you can give it right back."

"Another family heirloom?"

"This one my father doesn't care about. It's not quite as important as the ring." Another small shrug.

Carefully, I lift the lid. The moon shines off a necklace, meant to sit against my throat, lined with lavender stones and a single diamond pendant, hanging at the center.

"Malcom. This is beautiful." I close the lid. "I cannot accept this. Really, it is too much."

"You can't return a Yule gift, that's rude, and you don't strike me as the type that means to offend." He offers a half smile, tucks his hands in his pockets, and begins backing away. "Keep the necklace, Poesy. I'll see you at the ball. May all your holiday dreams come true."

"Thank you," I call after him.

He disappears into the woods, absorbed into the darkness, leaving me alone in front of my house with the finest piece of jewelry I've ever owned.

SONNET

The Calloways' home is bright with light. It pours out the front door and into their open drive. Those large iron gates Malcom and I had snuck through are wide open. A line of carriages waiting to get inside trail down the street. Even as the carriage approaches the front door, I can hear the music drifting out into the yard.

There's an energy in the air. An excitement that can't be contained and it is spreading to everyone who comes near. It races up into my body and mingles with the traces of guilt and nerves that run inside of me.

"Are you okay?" My father leans forward. The same dress clothes he wore for my mother's funeral have been brightened with a green undershirt and small silver cufflinks, a handmade project he'd done himself.

I try to school my features into the excitement that has been building in my chest for days. Yet, whatever expression I muster only makes my father's lips turn down. "I'm nervous, is all. Don't worry about me."

"Your mother would be very proud, I hope you know. You've taken on work that you never should have had to do and you've done it with a smile. Still, yet, you've managed to come out of mourning and dazzle the court." He reaches forward and pats my knee. His freshly polished wedding band glints on his ring finger. "I'm so very proud of you."

"Thank you," I say quietly back.

Our carriage finally comes to a halt in front of the Calloways' front door. Gravel crunches under my heels when Edmund offers me his hand and guides me out into the night. Garlands and winter berries have been wrapped around the railings leading up the small flight of stairs. Wreaths hang on both sides of the two open doors. The polished floors that I remember gleam with a fresh layer of wax. Pine trees have been cut and propped in nearly every corner of the entry room, each branch decorated with large red and white baubles.

"Are you ready?" Father asks at my side.

Together we look to the staircase leading up to the ballroom on the third floor. Other families in their expensive attire are already making their way up. Chatter and laughter guide us toward the party.

The Yuletide Ball.

It's finally here.

My hand trembles as I hook my arm around his. I can feel the light beading on my lavender gown through the thin white gloves as I hold my skirts up enough not to trip. Together we make our way up, my father the calm and confident presence next to me that I need.

Everywhere we look the home has been dressed for the holiday. It's as though we've walked into a piece of art. My heart flutters as I take it all in. The space smells warm like freshly baked cookies and cinnamon, with a hint of cranberries. Poinsettias brighten the room, their large red petals pleasant and docile.

On the third floor, it's as though the holiday has projectile vomited all over the room. Not a lick of space isn't devoted to Yule. Candles flicker in chandeliers dressed with more sparkling baubles. Strings of tinsel hang from every decorative branch artfully posed throughout the space. Couples already grace the large dance floor, spinning in blurs of gems and hues of red and green.

The doors to the ballroom are set open, the

Calloway Family standing a few feet inside greeting guests as they approach. Nervous bubbles form and burst in my stomach as I look over the people in front of us to catch a glimpse of Cassius. His suit is as pale as my dress, something I'm quite sure Edith arranged. The pale color of his undershirt makes his blue eyes appear even brighter. They stand out like light shimmering across water on a sunny day. His blond curls are neatly brushed away from his face, smoothed back and tamed in a way that makes him look as expensive as his home. As expensive as the ring I'd stolen from him. My stomach drops a little at that. Still, I walk forward with my father as if nothing is wrong, as if I don't feel moments away from turning and running from the one night I'd worked these last few months for.

When it's finally our turn to enter the ballroom, my father gives a stiff bow, the most he can manage with his back, and I curtsey deeply. As we both rise, Edith wraps me in a tight hug. The sweet scent of vanilla wafts around us.

"I'm so glad you could make it," she says, bearing a grin that reaches up to both of her pretty pointed ears.

"I wouldn't miss this for the world. How's your ankle?" I ask.

"Better than ever, thanks to Dr. Lowen."

Edith holds my hands and gives me the slightest squeeze before Cassius extends his hand in invitation.

"And your face?" I look up, examining his hair line while placing my palm in his. His hand is cool in comparison to Malcom's always warm touch. Where the bruises once were is smooth and blemish-free.

"Better than ever," he repeats his sister's sentiment before bringing my knuckles up to his mouth for a swift kiss. "Mr. Weatherwood." He looks to my side. "Might it be alright if I borrowed your daughter for a few dances?"

"It would be my honor." Then softer, my father whispers to me, "Have fun, my dear. If you need me I'll be right over there." He points to a table in the corner of the room and swiftly steps over to it, leaving me and Cassius alone to walk out onto the dance floor.

I meet the stares of more than one curious set of eyes as we walk together onto the dance floor. Apart from Trudy's holiday party, my family had not been invited to the other holiday events. Cassius and I had not walked hand in hand for any other party between then and now, making this almost feel as though it's the first time all over again.

In the sweeping of my attention, a dark brown gaze peers at us from the corner of the room. Malcom leans against a pillar, and a petite woman with brilliant red hair chats enthusiastically next to him, but he only watches me and lifts his glass in salute. I tip my head to him, smiling softly to myself, trying hard not to think about the practice kiss we shared.

Music picks up with a cheerful beat as dancers form their lines. I join across from Cassius, holding his gaze and noting the almost animalistic way he watches me. His eyes trail my gown, catching on my chest and hips. It's only when we start dancing and are finally brought together that he finally looks back up to my face.

"Edith was right; you look absolutely stunning in that dress."

I spin under his arm, the material fanning out around my legs. "Thank you. You look rather handsome yourself."

"But you are good enough to eat."

He winks, bringing me against his body. Everyone else separates into their lines again but the two of us remain close. A prickle of unease makes the back of my neck heat. I try to pull away gently, but his hold tightens. Though it's hardly proper, I must admit it does feel a little bit romantic to be tucked away doing our own thing, caught up in our own bubble. So I lift my face to his and smile despite the nagging feeling in the back of my mind.

"I'm hoping at the end of the night that you might stay with me a moment longer. As the host of this event, I'm expected to dance with many young ladies and will be stolen away to talk with guests. I'd rather be with you, but if you'd stay a bit longer we might get a second to ourselves. Then I can really show you how much I appreciate you coming as my date."

A second to ourselves. That is hardly enough time to get into any trouble. I'd hate to pull him away from his responsibilities of host. So I nod in agreement.

Cassius holds me for the remainder of the song. We sway, slightly off beat, until the music comes to an end. He gives me a shallow bow, presses one last kiss to my knuckles, and tells me to enjoy my night. Which I do. I dance with my father. I gossip with Trudy. I laugh with Edith. Most of all, I avoid Malcom and he avoids me. The necklace he gifted me, sits proudly on my neck. Often, I find myself brushing my fingers along the row of gems.

"You look like you could use a drink," Eames says offering me a glass of wine. Unlike his brother, his blond hair is cropped short, and two diamond stud earrings shine in his ears. His eyes widen a fraction as he catches my necklace. "*That* looks familiar. A gift from my brother?"

"It is." I take the wine and sip politely.

"Then why is it that you two are so close yet have been dancing around each other all night? If I have to watch him making those sad puppy dog eyes one more time I might drown myself in the punch bowl."

"He's not made any sad puppy dog eyes. I don't think he's even capable of that. Every time I've seen him he's just...glaring." Not in an angry sort of way but in the way that his face always looks as though he's mad when he's not trying to be charming.

"So you've been watching him." Eames smirks, the look nearly identical to the one I've seen his brother wear.

"No. Well." I take another sip. "I'm not watching him, but I have taken notice of his presence."

"Interesting." He hums as he bobs his head.

"Is it?"

"I think so. My brother has been a different man as of late. Not that you'll catch me complaining about it. I only find that it has correlated quite coincidentally with the sudden appearance of you in his life. And for that, I must thank you."

"I'm sure as you've said it is only coincidental." It must be.

"Well, you might not be able to tell the difference between his normal broody disposition and this pathetic display, but I sure can. He's watched you like a hawk all night, a sad, pining hawk." He lifts his glass, clinking it against mine. "Enjoy your drink, Miss Weatherwood. I do hope my family will be seeing more of you."

Then he's gone. He and his full black suit disappear into the crowd. As if I'm pulled by a string, I search out Malcom. Our gazes collide and is brows furrow before he turns away and follows after his brother.

No. Malcom doesn't have sad pining puppy eyes for me. He couldn't. We're both moving forward and the sooner we get through this bargain the sooner we can move on with our lives. The sooner I can move on with my life with Cassius.

It isn't until the ball is starting to wind down that I finally see Cassius again. He parts the crowd, everyone moving around him as though he's a hot knife passing through butter. Those stormy eyes snare me, drawing me forward. He takes my hand spinning me across the dance floor, though we never stop to stay in one spot.

"Finally, I've gotten away from my mother and all the others who wanted to chat my ear off. It's exhausting."

"Hopefully you're not too exhausted yet. The night's not over," I say, laughing as he twirls me out and then back in, playfully swaying with my back against his chest.

His face lights with what I can only describe as pleasant surprise. And then we stop. His chest rises in soft breaths against me as he turns me to fully look up at him. Someone next to us cheers. Someone else lets out a long, "Ooooo." Cassius looks up, and my breath snags when I follow his gaze.

The mistletoe. Pointed leaves and red berries on a fig perfectly hung with a red ribbon above our heads.

"It is tradition." He searches my face in answer as though he's asked a question.

"Tradition *is* important." I can hardly hear myself speak. Others have joined around us, laughing and cheering us on. Suddenly, getting kissed under a mistletoe doesn't feel so romantic anymore. It feels as though I'm once again the evening's entertainment and that's not a feeling I ever wanted to experience again.

Cassius takes my statement as his answer and lowers his mouth to mine. His hand wraps around the back of my neck, holding me hostage. His lips smash over mine, his tongue darting into my mouth to plunder and take without care. He even bends me backward, holding me tightly as he dips me back in a gesture that makes the room shake with excitement. The crowd shouts so loudly it rattles my bones.

Somehow I end up standing upright again, my hand in Cassius' as he holds our intertwined fingers up as though we've won something. And I feel *nothing*. There is no rush of holiday joy or the excitement the rest of the room is experiencing. There are no butterflies or tingles. No goosebumps. In fact, his hand is a little sweaty and I'm grateful when he finally lets me go.

"If you'll excuse me, I think I need a drink," I say in a hushed tone to Cassius. He hardly gives me a response as he gives me a wave and strolls right up to a group of guys ready to pat him on the back. All of it makes me feel worse. Somehow dirtier. Certainly wrong.

Where is the feeling of the holiday magic? One more thing has been checked off but it certainly doesn't feel *right*, let alone magical.

At the punch bowl an attendant spoons liquid into a cup for me and hands it over with a pitying look. My stomach does something then. It bunches uncertainly. No butterflies. No fun little flutters. Cramps. My stomach cramps. Drinking will help, I assure myself, tipping my cup and swallowing the contents in one gulp.

The crowd doesn't part for me like it does for Cassius. I pass through, slipping into any space I can find muttering 'excuse mes' and 'pardons' as I go. I only pause when I see Malcom in my path. His drink stills an inch from his face as he watches my approach.

"Malcom," I say in greeting, slowing my pace.

"Sonnet." He lifts is glass again. "Congratulations on getting everything you wanted. I believe our deal is done."

"That it is."

"Happy Yule, I guess." The smile he gives me is tense as he turns and strolls away before I can respond.

"Happy Yule," I whisper, mostly to myself.

SONNET

The Calloways' staff have taken to cleaning the perimeter of the room while the very last of the guests remain. Couples sway to the last band member who strums against his standing instrument. Those who are left stumble more than walk as more staff comes to whisk them toward the door.

"Miss Weatherwood," a tall slender man with a well-managed gray beard says, "Lord Cassius has asked that you be seen to his chambers."

His chambers?

"To his room?"

"Yes," he says, turning and walking away before I can protest.

I gather my skirt and hurry after him, passing the guests who stumble down the stairs to their carriages. With the promise that Melborn Calloway, Cassius' father, would keep an eye and act as chaperone, my own father had left at a respectable hour. Yet, Melborn had hardly been seen afterward. Cassius hardly either after our kiss. Once Edith retired and Trudy had gone home, I'd spent the majority of my time being bored right out of my wits. Eames had dropped off one last drink for me before even the Blacks had left, Malcom with little more than a glance in my direction. With our bargain ending what was left of our friendship is quickly fizzling out. Part of me is relieved by it while the rest of me wants to frantically cling to it.

Eventually the halls become recognizable. I can count the doors and I know exactly where the man is taking me before he even gets there. He opens the door, waving me in, and closes it right behind me. There is a fire in the hearth, warming and lighting the room. I turn, taking it all in, feeling in my bones how very alone I am.

No chaperones and now I'm in Cassius' room? No part of this feels right. It has to be my nerves. Anyone else would feel this way if they were in my situation.

You can leave whenever you want, Sonnet, I remind myself.

I busy myself looking at the books stacked on his desk, none of which are fiction or anything remotely of interest to me. I stand for some time in front of the painting I know opens up into the space I'd slipped through not so long ago and pull back his curtains to watch as the last of the carriages pull away. I do anything except think about how my body aligned so perfectly against Malcom's. Which is to say, that is all I can think about. No matter how much I pretend to care about Cassius' design choices, my mind always drifts back to *that*.

"Doing some snooping?" Cassius says from the doorway.

I jolt but manage to smile as I turn toward him. "What else was I to do with my time?"

He chuckles softly. The door snicks shut. "I do apologize for your wait. Official Yuletide business." His steps are slow and leisurely as he makes his way close.

"Ah, yes," I answer, "Yuletide business waits for no one. I understand."

"I knew you would." He reaches out and tucks his hand on the back of my neck, in the same fashion he had when we'd kissed before. "I've been thinking about you all night. That kiss."

Where I want to feel the tingling sensation of desire, I feel nauseous instead. "That was some kiss."

Cassius steps closer yet and I fight the urge to

step away at the same time. His breath smells strongly of wine. His face lowers over mine, his lips brushing against me before I turn away.

"Do you like to read? I see many books on your desk?" I ask, pointing behind me.

His mouth purses before he manages a smooth smile again. "Mostly reading material for my extended schooling. I don't really *read* for fun."

"What do you do for fun then?" What could be more fun than reading? In fact, I'd love to have more time so that I could get through more novels.

"Come." He takes my wrist gently in his hand and pulls me behind him. "Let's sit, relax." We stop at the edge of his bed and he lowers onto it, patting the space next to him that I'm meant to sit in. I lower into the spot my palms feeling slick. "You look so beautiful tonight, Sonnet."

"You can thank your sister for that." I laugh but it's dry and nervous sounding.

"Let's not talk about my sister." With his fingers spread wide, his hand flattens against my thigh. "I'd rather talk about us." His touch slides higher and I squirm, swallowing down my protest. This is Cassius. This is exactly what I wanted. To have his attention. To gain his affection.

"Us?"

"Mmhmm." He leans closer and I know he's going to kiss me. Malcom's words repeat in the back of my mind though I try my best to drown them out. This kiss is as rough as the last. There is no gentle give and take, nothing that sets my insides burning. It's merely the press of lips, rough and chaste.

"Cassius." I pull away. "There is hardly a mistletoe here."

"Oh, that's alright. We've no chaperone to scold us." That hand circles my hip, his fingers curling into the materials of my gown.

"Don't you want to talk and spend proper time together?" It's the naive part of me that wants this to turn around, to get back to where I hoped this could be.

"I don't want to talk. There are better things we could be doing with our mouths." His eyes flare but his grin remains.

Malcom's voice speaks a little louder from the back of my mind. *He's placing bets on what it would take to get you into his bed.* And here I am, in his bed, and he's making those eyes at me...his hand continuing to follow the curve of my body.

My body tenses. "To be clear, Cassius, you did not bring me here to *talk*."

"No. Why would I have them bring you to my bedroom to talk?" Lines form around his eyes, his features scrunching, but he otherwise holds his pleasant facade. That's what this is after all. A mask. One I've been dumb enough to fall for.

"For privacy, so we can be free with our words," I say, clinging to that last line of hope.

"For privacy, so we can be free with our *bodies*," he corrects, "No one is here to judge you, Sonnet. It's just me." His palm aligns against the side of my face, gently coaxing me forward.

"I'll be ruined," I whisper. I might already be ruined. All this time I thought I was playing them, that I was outsmarting the Court of Frost, yet it turns out that it's me who's lost this game. I should have never played to begin with.

"I won't tell a soul," Cassius swears. "This stays between us."

It won't. I know it won't. And every second I spend here alone unchaperoned will only make it all worse.

I stand, nudging his hand away from me. "I have to go."

"Sonnet." He grips my wrist tightly. "If you leave now, I'll never invite you back. You'll lose your chance at *us*."

"Take me home, Cassius."

"If you're leaving then you can walk," he scoffs.

There never was and would never be an us.

I chuckle softly and slip out of his grip,

allowing myself one last look at what I thought was supposed to be my dream. His perfect curls, those bright blue eyes, the magic, the family, the power...all of it. None of it ever truly mine to have or even within my reach.

Gripping my skirt, I run. The Calloways' staff must think me wild as I sprint through the halls both angry and sad, bitter and hurt. I stop long enough to grab my coat from a servant then throw myself out into the cold. The bite of the winter air is almost soothing to the frantic, throbbing, ache that floods my body. Tears sting at the corner of my eyes, freezing against my cheek as they fall.

I rip at the pins and ribbons holding my hair back, stripping away the pretty picture I'd painted for the court to see. The picture all of them saw right through. I don't have magic and they do. There's nothing that could change that. Nothing that could erase the line that's drawn between us.

What good is this gown, these jewels, the perfect arrangement of my hair if they're never truly able to see me? I've masked myself as much as Cassius. My stomach flips with the idea that I'm even remotely similar to him.

The night I've grown so accustomed to walking in surrounds me. Familiar sounds of branches rustling in the breeze, the occasional howl of a beast or coo of a bird, and the snapping of Bitten Woods calms my racing pulse. I slow my sprint only as I near the woods. I stumble to a stop when I turn the bend to find a man lying out across the snow. No cloak. No mask. Just white-blond hair and his dark brown suit.

I stay silent and he doesn't so much as move as I approach. Then with a sigh, I lower myself to the ground and lay in the dirt path right next to him.

SONNET

He could be painted like this, is the first thought I have as I lower myself onto the dirt and turn to look at his profile. The man himself could have been carved by an artist's hand from marble with his strong nose and chiseled chin. Muscles feather along his jaw as he stares up at the night sky.

Stars appear and then disappear behind a haze of clouds. Even the moon plays, casting its light down on us one moment and then hiding away the next. It's silent on the road that cuts through these woods. Only the sounds of nature and the hushed noise of our breaths as we lay still next to one another.

Malcom doesn't turn to face me, but he curls an arm up toward me, letting a finger graze against my coat. His power quickly fills my veins, fighting away the cold. I let him, savoring this moment where my hate softens and my sorrow is harder to find.

What would my mother think of me now? Would she be disappointed to find me sprawled out in the middle of a road, next to a criminal, but now a criminal myself? Soon I'll be the laughingstock of the court as Cassius will no doubt not stay quiet. I've given them enough evidence to support him anyway...letting him whisk me about the dance floor and tip me back into a dip as we kissed under the mistletoe.

Everything is wrong. Yet, I can't quite find it in myself to regret having stumbled upon Malcom in these woods or having hit him repeatedly with my bag. Though I could have struck him a few extra times for good measure. With the deal completed, we'll be on our separate ways. I can pretend none of this happened as I piece together my new life and forget about the goings on of court. Surely, a quiet life won't be so bad.

I sigh. I've never been one to want a quiet life. I enjoy the balls and the parties. No matter how shallow it feels to admit, I like the dresses and the jewels.

White clusters of snowflakes drift down from the sky. Still, neither of us dares to move or break this small bubble of solitude. Not even when the flakes start to gather on our bodies. Eventually, I'll have to speak up. But not now. Not yet.

The two of us lay like this, unmoving and uncaring, for what feels like hours. Malcom's powers keep us warm, though I wonder if it's beginning to put a strain on him. It's me who finally breaks the silence for fear that he'll over expend himself and not say a word.

"You were right." The night swallows the sentence.

He turns to look at me, eyes dark and hollow. "I didn't want to be right." The light touch of his finger moves as she strokes gently against my arm. "Did he hurt you?"

I look at him, watch as his throat bobs, and shake my head. "No, I left before anything could happen. Apart from my pride and my reputation, I remain...*intact*." Though rumors can do just as much damage. They pretend like my virginity is the end all be all of what I'm worth, but they won't care that I've saved myself because, to them, I'll already be ruined.

"I couldn't care less about the status of your virginity, Sonnet. If you were happy and willing, then the rest is none of my business, but if he hurt you..."

"You'd what?"

"I'd kill him," he whispers, turning to look

back up at the sky. His finger never stops its gentle, soothing strokes.

"Being a murderer is quite the leap from breaking and entering."

"It's a slippery slope, so I'm told."

I exhale a laugh. But to say that he'd hurt Cassius over me? I fear I've been fooled one too many times when it comes to men with magic and money. Malcom can as easily be pretending to be someone who cares for me. He and Cassius are more alike than he and I will ever be.

"Our bargain is over," I say, brushing the wispy strands of hair from my face and blinking against the cluster of snowflakes that have attached themselves to my eyelashes. "What do we do now?"

"What do you want to do, Poesy?"

Now that's the question. What do I want? For a while, I thought that all I wanted was the perfect holiday. I wanted the balls, the social life, the date, a kiss under the mistletoe...now it all feels so underwhelming. Perhaps distance from everything would be nice. Lest I forget that Malcom has magic, power, and the life that I'll never be able to have. Society will always be against us, even as friends. These past few months have taught me that. My wants might not be as important as what I need. So what do I need?

"What I want is not so important," I murmur, trying to memorize every dip and curve of his face. "Our deal is done. I think it's best if we go our separate ways, don't you?"

"It's for the best," he repeats, flatly.

I tip my head back up to the night sky. Even the woods fall silent around us as we lie on this dirt path, two lost people counting the stars. When his warmth begins to fade, he gently pulls his hand back. The cold wet snow that has soaked my fine gown makes every inch of me feel like ice. I exhale, cup my hands to catch my breath, and rub them together.

"Let me walk you home." Malcom rises. He extends his hand and I take it, allowing him to pull me to standing. We shiver for a moment as we stare at each other in quiet contemplation. I can't help but try to burn his image into my mind, knowing that after this we'll go back to hardly knowing each other. With my reputation ruined, I'll hardly be attending any events. Even Trudy might be a bit put out extending an invitation.

Malcom offers his elbow and arm in arm we take to the last of the path. My mind mulls over my memories. Of every time the court made me feel less than. Of the times Cassius flirted and touched me. Of every damn thing that had somehow gone wrong or not lived up to my expectations. Maybe I'm the problem. All these things have one thing in common and it's me. So it's time I take a step back. I'll figure it out eventually and even if I don't life will carry on anyway.

At the rickety gates of my house, Malcom turns toward me and extends his hand. "Our deal is complete. Thank you for helping me."

His grip is large and easily swallows mine as I shake his hand. "We should probably go on about our lives without each other now, I suppose."

"So this is goodbye?" The corners of his mouth tighten but don't quite turn into a smile.

"This is goodbye."

Malcom holds my stare for a heartbeat, then two, before turning and heading toward those fated woods. I push through the gate, hinges hissing.

"Sonnet?" Malcom calls, walking himself backward into the dark of night.

"Malcom?"

"I truly hope you have a wonderful Yule tomorrow." Not even an ounce of sarcasm or frustration stains the sentiment. My body warms by several degrees.

"You too, Malcom. Happy Yule." I give him a little wave.

And this will be the last time I see Malcom Black. Instead of the relief that should fill me, I find simply sadness in the wake of our bargain.

SONNET

The longest night of the year has come and gone. The early morning sun washes away the stars and moon in splashes of pink, orange, and purple. A fresh layer of snow sparkles across the lawn, dusting the curved details of our short iron gate and hiding the rust. It's easy to see the beauty in the world when I look at it from this angle. Perfect unblemished snow. A sunrise as a promise to banish away the cold of winter. My home filled with the scent of a fruit cake, baked in tandem by my father and sister. I smile to myself wondering if it's turned out or if we'll be eating fruit pancakes instead.

For a second, I hear Merry humming a holiday song outside of my bedroom, and it's easy not to think about Malcom. She sounds like Mother. If I close my eyes for a second, I can pretend that she's out there, but that only serves as a reminder that when I open them she'll still be gone. It's a bittersweet feeling as I tug my curtain closed and stretch before heading for the door. As it opens, Merry's humming stops and she straightens from where she's adjusting one of her handmade baubles she's hung on our tree. Though I see no future for her in baking, her baubles actually turned out quite nice. Perhaps one day she'll open up a holiday shop if she doesn't marry into a magical family.

"Happy Yule!" she squeals and sprints toward me with her arms open wide. "I'm so glad you're awake! Now we can open up our presents."

"Let your sister eat first, Merry." Father's tone is gentle but stern.

I laugh and hold Merry tightly, swaying one way and then the next, singing the song she'd been humming into her hair before whispering, "Happy Yule, Merry." We break apart only so that I can spin her about. She twirls away in her green dress, red ribbons tying back most of her hair as her dark strands fan out around her.

Floorboards creak and groan as she dances away and Father stands from his seat at the dining room table to press a kiss to both of my cheeks. "Eat so your sister can quit nagging me, please," he whispers, shaking out his napkin as he sits himself back down and places it in his lap.

"Is everything...edible?" To their credit, it all appears as it should. Nothing is flat. Nothing looks melted. Even the icing she'd spread across the cakes looks fairly well done. None of this is to mention the small spread of meat, cheese, fruits, and eggs that all cause my mouth to water and my stomach to growl loudly.

"I've not been poisoned yet." He shoves a bit of cake into his mouth.

"Yet," Merry repeats from across the room. "There's still time if you two don't hurry it up."

Laughing, I fill my plate and make a show of tasting each bite as I eye my sister with mock suspicion. Every moment we linger, Merry's eye twitches a little more and her sighs grow louder. All of which only feeds into my father's and my shared amusement.

"Wow," Father says as he leans back and pats his stomach. "Every year I'm so thankful for you girls." I don't miss how his eyes slide to the empty seat my mother always claimed at his side. The dull throbbing in my heart that's never really gone away pulses with newfound strength. "Happy Yule, girls."

"It's not a happy Yule until you both get over here to open up these presents." Merry comes to pull at our father's arm, forcing him to stand with a groan and a laugh.

I smile at their playfulness. Would Malcom be eating breakfast with his family this morning? Would anyone be telling him happy Yule? How strange it is that in our house the love, joy, and holiday spirit abound despite our heartaches, but in his home with all his riches and power there is none.

There is no need to think of Malcom, I scold myself. What relationship we've had is done. My holiday checklist is complete. His family ring is back in his home. And no one is the wiser.

And his family necklace he'd gifted me sits on display in my room. A glittering decoration I see before I go to sleep at night and again when I wake up. The only souvenir of our time together.

I rise from my seat to follow my family to our little tree. Merry's decorations have weighed down every branch making it look both sad and cheerful at the same time. Once our Yule tree had sheltered an abundance of gifts, all items we'd since either had to sell or had left behind when we'd been forced to move. Now our little tree only stands over a small sampling of wrapped boxes. Two for each of us. Simple. Modest.

My sister and I lower onto the floor, despite the perfectly fine furniture behind us, and Father drags over a chair to be next to us. Camping out on the living room floor has been a tradition for as long as I can remember. Though this year with Father's injury it's not easy for him to get up and down. Yet, an empty space remains, the spot where my mother should be. Though I like to think she's still here in spirit, watching, and grinning that wide goofy grin of hers.

"Me first." Merry snatches up her two wrapped gifts before shredding through the wrapping and ribbons in hardly a second. Hastily, she reveals the matching hat and glove set from me and a set of kitchen utensils hand-carved by my father. She squeals and holds the gifts to her chest before examining them more closely. "These are beautiful. Thank you so much Sonnet." She runs her finger over the carefully made floral design Father had etched into every handle and blinks back the moisture in her eyes. "Father, these are lovely. How did I never catch you making them?"

"These have been my little projects after you've gone off to bed." He smiles. Truly he might be able to make himself a new career with his recently found passion. And with the right tools.

"You next." I stretch forward and push the gifts toward him.

"No, you should go next, please. I insist." He and Merry both set their gifts in my lap.

Here I am, surrounded by my favorite people with two hard-earned gifts, and Malcom is probably in his home, sitting in silence, celebrating nothing. How sad. To redirect my mind from him, I slip my finger into the thin messily done wrapping.

"That one is from me." My sister claps her hands in excitement. "I hope you love it."

"I'd love anything you give me." The paper falls away to reveal a rectangular box.

"That's not true. You didn't like it that time I gave you a cold."

I laugh and lift the lid to reveal a pair of heels. The silken fabric that wraps them is a lovely shade of yellow and a collection of stones sparkle in the center of a small bow that sits on top of the toes. My jaw drops.

"Merry. These had to be out of budget. How on earth did you get them?" I'd slipped both my sister and father a small bundle of change to help them acquire any gifts they'd like to purchase. Somehow Merry had made her coin stretch farther than I ever thought possible.

"I have my ways. Do you love them?" Her eyes are wide staring at me waiting for my reaction. "I thought they'd be perfect since you're attending so many events now. Now you have nice shoes to go with your dresses."

The gold in the shoes reminds me of the sun-kissed dress Malcom bought me for Trudy's event. I close my eyes for a moment to hold back any emotions that might slip out before whispering, "I love them so much, thank you."

"You're welcome. Now the other."

Impatient, stubborn girl, but I do as she says, carefully setting down the pair of shoes and reaching for the small present from my father. His fits perfectly in the palm of my hand and when the wrapping is gone a velvet box remains. I open it carefully, somehow knowing something immensely valuable rests inside.

Two small pendant earrings, the same yellow as the shoes, like tears of liquid gold. I suck in a breath. I know these earrings. Mother's earrings from the portrait of them on their wedding day that hangs in Father's room.

In my silence, my father's throat bobs before he clears his throat. "I made sure to bring these with us when we moved. They were a little worn from time, seeing as they belonged to your mother's mother before. I melted down some metal and was able to reset them myself."

"I—" Emotion clogs my throat. Merry leans into my side, wrapping her arm around me to give me a little squeeze.

"You work so hard for us, Sonnet. You deserve to have nice things," she whispers before planting a kiss on my cheek.

"I love them," I finally manage to say.

"Happy Yule, Sonnet." My father grins, reaching out to squeeze my shoulder.

I sniffle and point to his gifts. "Your turn."

He opens a collection of playing cards, all designed and hand-painted by Merry. He takes his time fanning them out and admiring them all, giving Merry bits of praise that makes her smile stretch all the way up to her ears. Then he opens the set of wood carving knives I'd bought him and marvels at each one, rambling on and on about all the projects he'll work on with these and what each knife would work well for.

As a family, we sit together on the floor admiring our few small gifts and looking up at the Yule tree before us. The longest night of the year has come and gone and the winter will soon follow bringing us new warmth and sunshine. All year I'll wait for another Yule to come, another day that feels as though we've been given a fresh start despite the challenges that come in between. Another day to soak in all the love and joy my family can give.

"You stayed awfully late at the ball last night," Merry hedges, looking up through her long lashes at me.

"I wish I wouldn't have." I chuckle.

"I was quite shocked that you attended with Cassius. I expected to see you with Malcom since you two spent so much time together," Father interjects.

"I spent time with Cassius too." I know I sound defensive. In all honestly, I might have enjoyed my night more if it had been Malcom at my side rather than Cassius. Malcom wouldn't have pushed for anything I wasn't willing to give. We could have danced and brooded in the corner of the room, laughing to ourselves, with not a care in the world.

"But you actually like Malcom," Merry points out. "And Malcom really likes you."

"Malcom tolerates me," I correct. Merry and Father share a knowing look. "Wait—do you think he likes me?"

"Why else would the man be sending you gifts and showing up at your house?" Father tilts his head, watching me.

"That was nothing." I try to wave off the notion. It was all for our deal. Malcom played his part and he did it well. It's my own damn fault for...*oh gods*...falling for him along the way.

Merry sets her hand on mine. "Sonnet, the way he looks at you isn't nothing."

"He didn't take his eyes off of you the entire night," Father adds.

"We're just—" I start.

"Friends?" Merry finishes. "No, you're not.

And I, for one, think it's silly that you are both pretending otherwise."

"Why don't you go talk to him?" Father stands and offers me a hand up.

"It's Yule. I can't just run over there and interrupt his morning." Not that I imagine he's had much of one.

"There's no law against it." He shrugs.

"Oh, please go. And bring him back so I can show him that my cooking has improved. I made him his own loaf."

"You made him his own loaf?" I gawk at my sister.

"Yeah, and Dad made him a dagger."

I spin back to my father who's hardly done any blacksmith work since his injury. "How?"

"It took a while and a lot of breaks, but it was a small project. Malcom Black deserves it as thanks for being so good to our family. Now why don't you go get him so we can bestow upon him our gifts." He points me toward the door.

"Now?"

"Do you like him, Sonnet?" Merry rises, planting her hands on her hips. Her green eyes are wide and sparkling. And they see right through me.

"I—" Inhaling, I try again. "Yes."

"Go get him, then." Her hands rise and fall in exasperation as if I should have already been gone or already rushed out of the house this morning to bring him back.

I shouldn't. I couldn't possibly.

Still, I want to.

Should I?

"Quit arguing with yourself," Merry snaps. "Go get him."

Her words are enough to spur me into action. *Go get him.* All those feelings I've ignored. The flutter of nerves, the rush of having him near me, the thrill of having him kiss me, all of it floods my body, pushing me to move. I slip into my boots, sling a cloak over my shoulders, and rush right out the door into the snowy morning.

Malcom

The Black household is quiet on Yule morning. As it is every Yule.

Early morning sun pokes around the edges of my thick curtains as I dress myself for the day, thinking fondly of my bed and imagining crawling back into it. My father wouldn't be pleased by that at all. Successful men rise early to greet the day; they do not laze about, as he says. Even on Yule. The man is truly the worst.

What must it be like to wake up in Sonnet's home on a holiday such as this? How does one's family spend time together and not feel painfully awkward and dreadfully bored? It's easy to draw up images of the family swaying and singing together like a damn children's book. And it hurts to know that some part of me wants that and may never get it.

I cuff my sleeves and reach for the doorknob. Stepping out into the hall, I listen for any signs of life. I doubt anyone is still sleeping yet you could hear a pin drop rooms away. Silence makes my ears ring. This damn house is always quiet, except on the rare occasions we host. Those are the only time the family lets loose.

A maid scurries quietly down the hall, a spare sheet held tightly in her arms. She slows at my approach, dipping into a slight curtsey. "Good morning, Mr. Black. Happy Yule."

"Happy Yule," I mutter in response, heading for the stairs then straight to the smaller, much less formal, dining room.

Unlike the Weatherwood's house, there is not a single decoration strung up. If I did not keep a close eye on the calendar days I would not know that today's a holiday at all. There was a time when I was a young boy when I'd been saddened by my family's lack of enthusiasm for Yule. That time when other young people spoke of what they wished they'd find under their trees. I'd come home certain my parents would put up a tree in the night and it would be filled with gifts. It was heartbreaking to wake up and find my parents hardly cared for the holiday at all. When asked, Father said, "It's just another day, Malcom." Somehow, the excitement still came every year and every Yule my heart would break all over again. Now only bitterness resides in my hollow heart.

Only one thing has made my heart feel as though it's beating again. One person. And like the fool I am, I've let her go. It's what she wanted but it still stings.

Part of me remembers Sonnet's invitation to join her family and longs to go. I do my best to ignore those longings. Sonnet is...happy. She got her holiday. And she doesn't need me there to muck it up. Just like I've ruined everything else.

Our family's dining room is dressed for breakfast only. Empty plates sit before our usually claimed seats and steaming trays of food await. Only Eames is at the table with a book in one hand and a fork shoveling food into his mouth in the other. He pauses as I enter, giving me the slightest nod before turning back to his book.

Lowering into my chair, one of our abundant ever-changing staff members comes to the table. I point to the food I'd like, letting them make my plate for me. Once I'd tried to learn the staff's names. As I grew and the frequency of their ever-changing faces grew, I stopped. As it turns out, my father is not an easy man to work for. Neither am I.

"Good morning, Eames," I say, picking up my fork and pushing at the food on my plate. "Where are our lovely parents on this fine day?"

"Said something about business..." His blond brows pull together. "Or something else. I don't know, Malcom. You know I stopped listening to them eons ago."

I hum my agreement, picking up my glass of water. The glistening rim reminds me of the way my family's ring glowed in Sonnet's palm. The same rise and fall of excitement and terror crests in my stomach at the thought. Sonnet was supposed to be a solution to my problems. I wasn't supposed to fall in love with her. Wanting her was fine. To see a creature as beautiful as her and to lust after her is acceptable. I'd happily take her to my bed if she was interested. Loving was supposed to be out of the question.

The moment that ring foretold of its wearer, she became mine. Though, I'd not tell her a lick of that if it is Cassius she wants. I'll sit in my own pain and misery forever to see her happy. No one ever said the ring couldn't be wrong or that the future couldn't be changed. It was she who had suggested we go our separate ways; that whatever portion of our lives we were to spend together is done. I'll let her have what she wants. I'll give her that distance, but I won't stop watching her or caring for her and her family however I can without notice.

"What's with the pouty look?" Eames asks, lowering his book. "You aren't still holding out hope that our parents will jump out to surprise us with all the holiday cheer their emotionless bodies can muster, are you?"

"No." I snort. "That shipped sailed forever ago."

His eyes narrow. "Is this about Sonnet?"

I swallow but don't answer.

"That was a wicked kiss Cassius gave her at the Yuletide Ball. Downright claiming her in front of the entire town. Though we all know he wouldn't marry someone of her standing. I wouldn't doubt that he plans to keep her around as a future mistress though. Who do you think won his bet?"

My grip around my fork tightens, both my hands curling into white-knuckled fists. I slam my hands on the table. "Shut your mouth."

"Oooo..." He smiles. "I see that I've hit a sore spot. I knew the long face had something to do with her." Eames shakes a finger at me. "I saw her in that necklace, and I knew you loved her. And here I was thinking you would never stop whoring yourself about and settle down."

All the blood drains from my face. My brother only smiles wider as he watches me.

"Everyone sees it but you two. Even Cassius who's happy to make your life a living hell. I wish you could have seen the look on your face when he danced her right under that mistletoe. I thought you were going to throw up everywhere or your eyes would pop out of that thick skull of yours. Honestly, this has been the most entertainment I've had in years, but it's clear you need a little push in the right direction now. Unlike Cassius, I don't wish to see you suffer long-term. Despite our family's inability to say it, I do have a love for you, my brother, and I want to see you doing and feeling well."

"She told me last night that it is best if we go about our lives without each other. I must respect her wishes. My feelings are a moot point." The metal fork glows red and wilts in my hand where power surges. I pull my arms back and sigh at the singe marks I've left on the wood. I'll be hearing about this later.

"That's odd."

"Is it?" I grind out through clenched teeth.

"It's only that she sent a gift over for you."

My heart does that ridiculous flopping in my chest that it always does around her. "A gift?"

Eames waves over one of the staff who approaches with a small box. He slides the present, wrapped in light blue paper the color of

Sonnet's eyes and tied up in a navy bow, onto the table.

"Does she know that you care for her? Because it is very apparent that she cares for you."

"I helped her. Did I not?" I stare at the box, unable to so much as reach for it. My body is rigid, frozen in my seat. "I've bought her gowns, given her gifts, visited her home, walked her from work every night. How could she not know that I *care* for her?"

"Did you say it?" Eames rolls his eyes.

"It was obvious." I drop my now curved fork to the table with a clatter.

"Did. You. Say. It?" my brother pushes, a brow raised.

I never said it. Not once. At least not with the implication that what is between us might be more than friendship. I shake my head slowly and Eames hums.

"You've got to say it, Malcom, or else she won't know for certain. The girl is not a mind reader, you know. Now open that, I'm curious what our first ever Yule gift in the Black house looks like." He leans forward. "Come on. I've been waiting for you to come down just for this."

If Eames notices the way my hands tremble as I reach for the small box, he doesn't say anything. Emotions rise like a tidal wave in my chest, clogging my throat. I tug gently at the ribbon, setting it aside, before tearing at the paper. A small white box sits underneath. Exhaling, I lift the lid.

A heartbeat passes and I can't move. All I can do is stare and stare. Eames stands from his seat trying to get a look inside.

"Well? What is it?" he demands.

I reach inside and pull the present out, holding it up for him to see. The small wooden soldier with its uniform painted in the colors of the Court of Frost. A little sword is poised in its wooden hand and I touch my finger to the end. It pricks against my skin, sharp but not sharp enough to make me bleed. I smile.

Inside the box, a bit of parchment is folded neatly with my name scrolled across it. Hand-drawn snowflakes decorate the edges of the page. I set the soldier down only to unfold the paper.

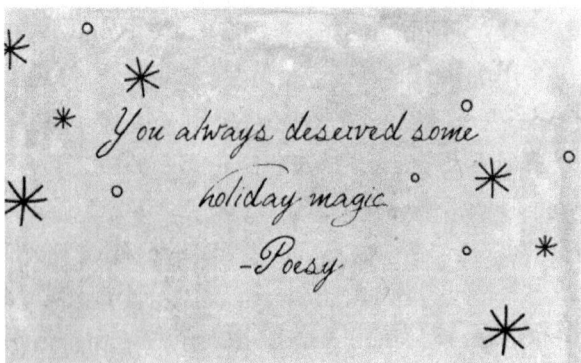

You always deserved some holiday magic

-Poesy

Poesy. My Poesy. Mine.

My chair hisses over the floorboards as I stand. For once, my brother might be right. She's not a mind reader; she doesn't know my feelings for her. There is a chance I might find myself a Yuletide miracle after all these years.

"Does this mean I'll be spending Yule alone, I hope?" Eames props his chin on his hand and bats his eyelashes at me. "You do know I love to have the house to myself."

"Would you be mad—"

"No! Go!" Eames waves me off with a flick of his wrist. "Is it not obvious that I'm trying to get you to leave? Get out of here. Go get Sonnet. Kiss her better than Cassius did and make everything right in this world again. If I must listen to that man gloat for one more day, I'll rip my own ears off. Trust that this is as much for you as it is for me."

I stare at him for a moment before he widens his eyes in urgency at me and I catapult myself into motion. Turning to the staff, who wait quietly against the wall, I point to the soldier. "Have this brought to my room and placed on my bedside table." I don't wait for so much as a dip of their chins before I spin toward the door.

The only sound that can be heard throughout our home now is the clip of my steps as I rush to leave, and somewhere behind me, Eames takes to humming a holiday song I only know vaguely. I pause at the door only to shrug into a jacket before taking off into the day. A white winter greets me. Not even the ice falters my steps. Nothing slows me until I reach the Bitten Woods.

Until I see her.

SONNET

S now falls in a torrent of white that obscures my vision. In my haste, I'd left my hair down and the wind whips mercilessly at my strands. Great, so I'll show up at his house looking completely ragged. I'm sure I'll be well received by his family. I can already imagine that the same mousey man who'd answered the door before will walk me right into the sitting room that's not actually for sitting again.

Only my determination outweighs that of my nerves. Why should I be nervous anyway? It's only Malcom. Immediately, my mind plunges into dark thoughts of his outright rejection. What if he laughs in my face? What if they all laugh in my face? Worse yet, what if they don't even let me inside? It would be nothing to his family to have the door shut right in my face. Still, I trust my family and if they believe he cares for me, I'm willing to take the chance. *If I even make it there*, I think, as my coat blows away from my body and my fingers turn to ice.

In the snow, ice, and sunlight, the Bitten Woods has gone from haunting and creepy to a regular winter wonderland. The trees look more like sculptures made of crystals than anything. Even the flowers, regularly active and hungry at night, are curled into themselves, their petals still and frost glistening over them. Any other time I might stop to admire the beauty of it but not today. Today I'm going to find Malcom and I'm going to tell him how I feel. And if I get hurt... well...I'll figure it out just as I've figured most everything else out along the way.

The dirt path through the woods is hardly visible through the accumulation of snow. With every step I take, I sink a couple of inches and have to yank my foot out to keep going. More snow still steadily falling around me. Cold sweat collects along my spine.

Through the snowfall, I see the bundled shape of a man appear. Snow has fallen so thoroughly over his head all I see is white. No. Not snow. Hair. White hair. The white-blond hair of Malcom. He looks up from where he was focused on the path seconds before our eyes lock.

A spark shoots through my entire being. That scar on my hand tingles and instinctively I brush a finger over it.

Both of us stand still, staring as our breathing clouds in front of us. Malcom is as handsome as ever, in that perfectly put-together yet somehow disheveled way. His hair sticks up at odd angles, blown back from his face by the wind. Pink darkens his cheeks, his brown eyes blazing as he stares at me. What is he thinking?

The fog quickly disappears as I forget to breathe. My chest aches in a pleasant needy way that masks the worry of rejection. Long bits of my hair blow across my features, but I don't move to fix them. All I can do is stare. And want.

Fierce desire courses through me. Everything that I've ignored or pushed away dares announce itself again. A fire burns low in my core, hopeful and needy.

Why is he out here? My stomach flips, hoping it's what I think. Begging the gods to let it be what I want.

Malcom moves first. He stalks forward, hands shoved deep in his pockets, the collar of his coat standing on end to block the wind. He's gone several steps before I'm able to force myself to move. When we finally meet, I have to lift my chin to hold that steady gaze.

"Why?" Malcom asks, roughly.

"Why?" I repeat, my attention searching his face for meaning.

"Why did you get me a Yule gift, Poesy?" His eyes are almost glassy as he asks.

I swallow, trying to appease my suddenly dry throat. Did he hate it? Is he mad? Am I totally wrong in thinking that he'd come all this way to see me and really he's only come to tell me off?

"Everyone deserves a gift on Yule," I whisper.

He shakes his head. "Why did you get me a gift?" he repeats.

"Did you not like it?" I slide my hands up into my sleeves, trying to hide my fisting hands. I'm going to be sick. He might reject me after all. Oh, gods, I am an idiot.

Malcom steps closer, forcing me to crane my neck to keep direct eye contact. "Answer the question, Sonnet." His voice is rough as gravel, grating over every sensitive nerve in my body, creating a shiver that runs through my being the way only he can.

"Because. Because I—I care, I suppose," I stumble over the admission, and it isn't even as grand as how I feel. Because shouting that I might very well love him here in this forest feels too vulnerable. Too scary now that we are face to face.

His gaze moves over my face, taking in every bit of my features. "Is that it?"

"Well, why did you get me a gift?" I fold my arms over my chest. Not only did he get me a gift but he'd given me another family heirloom. One less valuable than what we stole, I'm sure, but important nonetheless.

The corner of his mouth twitches. "Because *I* care. I more than care. Somehow you've made this lifeless heart of mine beat again. It's been a long time since I've felt joy during Yule and you've made this holiday the best thing to ever happen to me. Sonnet Weatherwood..." He gently pinches my chin, holding my head in place. "You're the best thing that has ever happened to me and I've fallen for you. Please tell me you feel the same way. If you don't I might very well perish."

I blink, certain I'm confused or that I've heard it all wrong. He's saying everything I wanted and now that I'm hearing it I'm not sure that it's real. By the gods, I want it though. Every part of me tingles with excitement.

"Say something," he whispers, his face lowering over mine, our lips an inch apart.

"I more than care too," I say the words on an exhale. "I'm falling for you, Malcom Black. I'm falling and I'm terrified you'll break my heart."

His eyes flutter closed, his mouth finally lifting into something of a smile. "I fear it is you who holds the power here. There is nothing that can be done to keep me from loving you."

Love.

After meeting on this path. After changing the course of both of our lives.

And after denying any sort of attraction along the way.

Somehow, we've gotten here. Love.

My heart feels so full it may burst.

His lips brush against mine. "If we cross this line, you're mine, do you understand?"

Oh, to be his. To belong to *the* Malcom Black.

"Only if that means you're mine too," I whisper back.

"Is that a deal, Sonnet Weatherwood?"

"I should know better than to enter into another bargain with a thieving fairy, but I'll swear it with a blood oath if necessary."

"What about with a kiss instead?"

"Deal."

The word has hardly left my mouth before Malcom's lips are on mine. One hand sinks into my hair, cradling the back of my head, the other wrapping around my waist and tugging me tightly against him until all the air between us is gone. There is no gentleness to this kiss. No soft caresses that build into more. This kiss is the buildup of every emotion both of us have fostered over the past couple of months. This kiss is the pouring out of suppressed feelings, unbridled lust, and the intense need to claim.

Malcom Black is mine. And I'll happily be his.

Perhaps all I needed to have a little bit of holiday magic is him.

Breathless, we break apart and I can't help my goofy grin. Unlikely partners in crime to friends to this. Only one thing could make me happier. I slip my hand into his, intertwining our fingers.

"Come back to my house with me," I say, reaching up to stroke my thumb across his jawline.

"So you can ravage me, I hope." He playfully nips at my hand.

"Better."

"Better than a proper ravaging?" He laughs, the sound echoing around us. "I don't know about that."

"Merry and Father have gifts for you. Come celebrate Yule with us."

Malcom goes still. "More gifts? For me?" I nod and a slow grin warms his face, his lips still crimson and swollen from the kiss. "You're spoiling me, Poesy."

"For years to come, I hope."

"For centuries to come." Malcom presses a kiss to my forehead before hand in hand we walk along the dirt path back to my house to celebrate the holiday that brought us together. There's enough magic in the air that for the day I don't even notice that I myself have no magic at all.

BONUS CHAPTER

Thank you so much for spending the holiday season with Sonnet & Malcom! If you're not a reader who enjoys spice this is the perfect place to stop. However, HAPPY HOLIDAYS to anyone who does. Please enjoy bonus Chapter 25.....

SONNET

The red dress fitted to my body feels more scandalous than anything I've ever worn before. It earned me several scowls throughout the night from more than one prim and proper lady. What did they expect from a party at the Blacks? The family is notorious for hosting events that darken into wicked delights and outright chaos. Each judgmental stare was worth it, if only so I could see Malcom's hungry gaze locked onto mine.

A stirring of something mischievous and sensual turns inside of me as I take his hand and let him lead me from the ballroom. Music muffles as the doors behind us close. Moonlight brightens the expanse of the yard beyond the balcony that remains cast in shadows. Brisk evening air circles the space but doesn't touch us as Malcom's warmth thrums through both our bodies.

Beyond the doors, the few party goers who have dared to stay late are dancing in what I might only describe as a drunken heap on the ballroom floor. And it's not so much dancing as it is swaying or grasping onto the nearest fairy to hold them upright.

"Poesy. My Poesy." Malcom walks me backward until my back hits the balcony railing. I tremble, though it's pleasant, as he cages me between his arms and runs his nose along the side of my neck. He breathes me in and hums.

"Tonight was a success, I think," I say quietly, tipping my head back to give him better access as he presses his lips against my flesh.

"Undoubtedly." His voice vibrates against me.

From meeting his parents—officially—to attending as Malcom's date—also officially—everything has gone off quite splendidly. Though my favorite part was witnessing Cassius' face when he watched us dance the night away together. Neither of us took other partners. Neither of us bothered to care about much of anything past the nearness of our bodies and the whispered conversations we held. Eames did try to cut in at one point but was promptly scared away by the rabid look that overcame Malcom at the mere mention of it.

It's a similar wild look that's taken hold of him now. One that I feel all the way into my bones.

"Do you think your parents like me?" I ask.

Malcom pauses his line of kisses to pin me with an amused look. "Do you think I care what my parents think?"

I reach up and wind my fingers into his hair, reveling in the silky texture. "I care what your parents think."

"They like you." He nods and I narrow my eyes in suspicion.

"You swear it?"

"Cross my heart and hope to die." A kiss is pressed to the tip of my nose. "Speaking of parents, does your father know you've come to a Black party dressed like a wicked little heathen?"

I start to smile but dig my teeth into my bottom lip to stop it. "What he doesn't know won't hurt him." And Edmund won't tell a soul. Another reason I love the older man. He came as my chaperone and with one quiet ask, happily stayed with the carriage waiting for the night to end instead of hovering inside the ballroom to keep an eye.

"I fear my evil ways are rubbing off on you."

"Maybe." I shrug.

Every breath I take, my breasts threaten to spill themselves from my low neckline. Malcom's eyes trail down from my face, catching the movement, before they tick back up to my gaze.

"What other terrible things can you teach me?" With a bravado I've never felt before, I run my hands down his body, hooking my fingers into his waistband and pulling him closer.

"Sonnet...don't tempt me. I do try and play nice for your sake but make no mistake that every fiber of my being wants to take you here and now up against this railing."

My breath catches in my chest. Desire lances through me, hot and demanding. I press my thighs tightly together, arching up against him.

"Maybe I want that," I whisper.

Malcom pulls away, watching me with intense scrutiny. "How much have you had to drink?"

I laugh and the sound echoes across his empty yard. "Two glasses of wine nearly two hours ago."

"Are you being serious or is this a joke?"

"Well, it wouldn't be a very funny joke. And considering jokes are supposed to be funny, that would mean this isn't a joke at all," I say. He blinks, eyes darkening. "I'm more concerned that we will be caught."

"We won't." His voice has turned to gravel.

The knot in his throat bobs. "I'll have you, if you'll have me."

Though my face is heated with a blush, I tremble with excitement. How many times have I imagined him? Too many to count.

I dip my chin in agreement, but he shakes his head. "I need to hear you say it out loud, Poesy. What do you want me to do?"

"Take me." I can hardly hear myself speak but the corners of his mouth tilt upward.

"Fuck you?"

"Fuck me," I repeat a fraction louder.

"Happily." Hot and impatient his mouth covers mine. Our kisses are a familiar well-trodden path at this point, but that doesn't make them any less exciting. His tongue parts my lips in one sweep before coming to parry with my own. Every caress sends a blistering heat coursing through me, all the way down to my curling toes.

His hand brushes along the curves of my body, leaving goosebumps in its wake. I gasp into his mouth as his finger grazes across my budding nipple. I do my own exploring, hands clumsily feeling over every dip of his muscular form.

"How well do you care for this dress?" he pulls away to rasp.

I find the buttons of his shirt, plucking them open one by one. "I do care for it a little." It is rather pretty. "But mostly, I can't walk back into the ballroom without it."

"Damn," he hisses under his breath, "I'd love to rip it off you."

My stomach flips. These are the throws of passion, the need to be so close to one another that every barrier between us is removed, even if violently.

"But..." he continues, speaking between the trail of kisses leading down my jaw, neck, chest, and then stomach. "I will endeavor to leave the gown intact."

I tilt my head back reveling in the sensation of his mouth perusing my flesh. A fresh current of air meets my legs, easily going through my stocking, and I look down to find Malcom kneeling before me, my dress lifted.

"What are you doing?" I whisper. While I'm innocent enough not to know every aspect of how this whole thing should work, I am aware that the parts of him that should be inserted into the parts of me are not currently lining up.

"Kissing you."

"Kissing—oh." I suck in a breath as he removes all barriers between my sex and him out of his way, tucking himself underneath the fabric of my dress, and his breath tickles the curls there.

He hums in what I hope is approval, or want, the sound a guttural noise that sends a thrill through me. Then his mouth is upon me. His tongue parting me and circling my sensitive bundle of nerves. I lean against the balcony, gripping its edges tightly, as sensations swell with every stroke he makes. If I don't hold on, I fear my body may take flight.

"Fuck. Sonnet." He growls against me, the vibrations nearly tipping me over the edge. "Fuck you taste so good."

Ecstasy, in such a concentrated form that I've not known before, rips through me and I cry out. His mouth doesn't stop its perfect motion until the sensations die down. When he rises, moisture glistens on his face and he pauses only to lick his lips like he just finished the most fantastic meal.

I swallow, loving every second of watching him. With his shirt unbuttoned, he's every part the rakish fairy I thought him to be. Only now he's my rakish fairy.

Needy for more, I grip his belt and pull him against me. His kiss tastes like my own liquid want and I groan against him. The metal of his belt jingles softly between us as I work to undo it and the fastening of his pants. When I'm finally able to unsheathe him and hold him in my hand, I pull away to marvel at such a manhood. I have no names for the strange yet beautiful parts of him. His most private area exposed before me, another layer of trust given between us. I circle my fingers around his length and his eyes flutter closed.

"How can I give you the same pleasure?" I ask quietly, suddenly a bit uncertain.

"I promise, anything you do to me will give me pleasure." He smirks before circling his own hand around mine and guiding me along his length. Back and forth our hands move in tandem. After a couple of leisurely pumps, his hand falls away letting me work the same movements on my own. But Malcom had not just touched me with his hand, he'd worked me into a tizzy with his mouth.

The fabric of my gown sighs as I lower before him and his eyes snap to mine. "You don't have to do that."

"I want to." I smile quickly and turn my attention back to his manhood. For a moment, I only look as I stroke him, slowly gathering the courage. I start by leaning forward, trailing my tongue over the beading liquid at the tip. Malcom moans. The sound is an encouragement and I want to pull more out of him, so I suck the tip into my mouth and take him until I'm gagging. He tastes mildly salty. Curling my lips around my teeth, I work him with my mouth the way my hands did moments ago. So near, Malcom smells like man, musk, and what I imagine sex might smell like. Something different but not entirely unpleasant.

Encouraged by the way his body tenses and the noises coming from him, I don't stop until he sinks his hands into my hair and forcefully pulls me back. "If you don't stop, I'll spill myself on your tongue."

"Do you not want to?" I bat my lashes at him and his eyes narrow in a mockery of sternness.

"Oh, I want to. Trust, Sonnet, I very much do. And if that's all you'll have of me tonight I'll be happy. But if you want..." His eyes darken. "... if you *have* me then I will wait."

Yes, having. That is what I want. If he spills himself in my mouth is there no having to be had though? So in this, I trust.

"Okay," I agree.

"Stand up." He rasps, tugging me up with a gentle pull of my hair. It's not rough enough to truly hurt but it's enough to have my full attention. The moment I'm up, he's gathering my skirts up and nudging my legs apart.

I let out a shaky breath and he locks eyes with me. "This may feel uncomfortable. It may even hurt, but it won't last long."

"Okay," I say again.

"I love you." He holds my gaze with an intensity that feels as though he's able to see straight through me.

"I love you." I nod.

"Sonnet, listen to me, I'm going to fuck you as though I don't. You were right about me. You've always been right. I'm terribly wicked and selfish. And I don't think once I'm inside you I'll have much control of myself. Do you understand?"

I nod again.

"Say it," he grinds out through clenched teeth.

"I understand."

Then in one thrust, he seats himself fully within me. A gasp rips through me, my body tensing with the sudden stretch and momentary achy pain. I tremble, wrapping my arms around his neck to hold myself as he grips my hips and slams into me again.

"Poesy. My fucking Poesy. You're so wet for me. So damn tight." He growls, the movement of his hips building speed. Each thrust slowly washes away the pain and replaces it with pleasure.

My body bounces against the railing, his arms anchoring me as he grinds into me again and again. Another wave of bliss rises with his movements. His panting breaths blow against my sensitive flesh. He pauses only to pull down at my dress, exposing my breasts to the night. They bounce heavily each time he enters me. The cold is quickly abated as his mouth meets the peak of one breast and he sucks it into his mouth, sending a shock that spikes a euphoric sensation straight to my core. His teeth graze over my nipple and I'm sent right back into that brilliant sensation that has me arching up into him.

His warmth leaves my chest. His hand circles my throat, putting pressure on either side that makes my head go light and lovely all at once while he works himself violently inside of me. My body jolts with every thrust but he holds me in place, secure in this realm though I'm quite sure my soul is ready to visit another.

Malcom moans as his body frantically pounds against mine and then tenses. Warmth spills within me and after another second he comes to a stop and rests his forehead against mine. Sweat has gathered along his brow, but I don't mind so much as we pant against each other.

"I'm sorry. You'll be sore tomorrow," he says quietly before pressing a kiss against my temple. He smiles a little, pulling himself free of me and immediately I miss every place we were connected.

"Don't be sorry. I enjoyed myself."

"You might think differently tomorrow." A

pained expression passes over his face before he looks away and rights his pants and belt. He pulls a handkerchief from his pocket and lowers before me, lifting my skirts to wipe at the dampness that's dripped down onto my thighs. "There is less blood than I imagined."

Is there blood? My eyes widen. "Is blood normal?"

He nods. "Yes, I only expected there to be more."

Is that a bad sign? Surely not. Nothing bad could have come from what we did when it felt so very good.

"Have you lain with many virgins?" I ask, though I'm not sure I want the answer for fear of the jealousy that might burn within me.

He bites his lip to suppress a grin. "Evil as you may think me, I do not go around taking maidenheads. You are the first."

Something in my chest relaxes, and I can't help but smile as he puts all my clothes back in place before tucking his handkerchief back in his pocket. He extends his hand and I take it, allowing him to put me back on his arm.

"You know, Sonnet Weatherwood. Of all the Yule gifts I received, I think you were the very best one. Come now, shall we take a stroll together on this fine evening?"

"That sounds lovely. Where to?"

"I know this nice little path, it's not very well traveled, but you do have a lovely scenic view through the Bitten Woods..."

REBECCA GREY IS A CHRISTMAS LOVING LADY THROUGH AND THROUGH. SHE LEADS A BUSY LIFE AND SOMEWHERE BETWEEN RAISING TWO KIDS AND DAYDREAMING ABOUT DECORATING HER TREE WHILE WATCHING CHEESIE HALLMARK CHRISTMAS MOVIES, SHE WRITES. AS A READER SHE ENJOYS BOOKS FILLED WITH BROODY LOVE INTERESTS, AND LARGE FANTASY OR PARANORMAL NOVELS. NOT TO MENTION HOLIDAY BOOKS! MUCH OF HER LOVE FOR THESE THINGS IS REFLECTED IN HER WRITING.

Also by REBECCA GREY

Awakened Fates Series

Crown of Blood & Glass

Dawn of Fate & Valor

Wings of Sunfire & Darkness

The Wings & Witches Series

A Cursed Hunt

This Fallen Fate

The Prince's Games Duology

Vengeance

Vanquish

Holiday Reads

Whims of the Wicked

Brothers of the Otherworld Standalones

Chasing Boston

The Darkest Queens Series

Made From Death

Kill The Queens

End Of The Sword

The Last Royal

Ruined By Fae Saga

Ruined

Madness

Heartsick

The Cursed Kingdom Series

The Cruel Fae King

The Cursed Fae King

The Crowned Fae Queen

The Twisted Crown Series

The Shadow Fae

The Iron Fae

The Lost Fae

Printed in Dunstable, United Kingdom